Your employer must see some unease on your face, because she smiles reassuringly and reaches down to pat your shoulder gently. "There's nothing to worry about."

At six foot seven, with the build of an Olympian, she's a reassuring presence. She's right, no mugger on Earth is going to voluntarily attack She-Hulk. "Thank you, Ms Walters. I'm fine. It's just... atmospheric."

"It certainly is, and please, do call me Jen."

"I will," you promise. Again. You remind yourself it's OK to be slightly rattled that you're walking through a notoriously sketchy murder-park in the middle of the night with a full-on super hero who has hired you as her in-state paralegal and local advisor.

To think you expected this to be a slow week...

ALSO AVAILABLE

MARVEL MULTIVERSE MISSIONS

SHE-HULK
Goes to
MURDERWORLD

TIM DEDOPULOS

ACONYTE

FOR MARVEL PUBLISHING

VP Production & Special Projects: Jeff Youngquist
Associate Editors, Special Projects: Caitlin O'Connell & Sarah Singer
Manager, Licensed Publishing: Jeremy West
VP, Licensed Publishing: Sven Larsen
SVP Print, Sales & Marketing: David Gabriel
Editor in Chief: C B Cebulski

First published by Aconyte Books in 2022

ISBN 978 1 83908 159 0

Ebook ISBN 978 1 83908 160 6

Cover art by David Nakayama • Interior art by Xteve Abanto
Technical assistance by Jonathan Green • Book design by Nick Tyler

Distributed in North America by Simon & Schuster Inc, New York, USA
Printed in the United States of America
9 8 7 6 5 4 3 2 1

ACONYTE BOOKS

An imprint of Asmodee Entertainment Ltd

Mercury House, Shipstones Business Centre

North Gate, Nottingham NG7 7FN, UK

aconytebooks.com // twitter.com/aconytebooks

HELLO!

This is an adventure gamebook. If you don't know what that is, maybe flick on through the next few pages for a moment, then head back here…

Yep, that's right, lots of numbered entries. You start at entry **1**, but must then decide which numbered entry to turn to next, according to what the text tells you. You do not just plough straight on to read the next page in order. Not because it's secret, but because it'll be really confusing, and that's no fun. We want you to have a good time.

In this adventure, you take on the role of She-Hulk's paralegal assistant as she investigates a case that keeps getting more complex. In addition to making decisions as part of an ongoing assessment for a permanent role, you are going to need to keep track of some stuff and roll some six-sided dice. So grab paper and pencil, or open up a text file, and track down a six-sider or two.

You have three core statistics in this book: **POWER**, **CHARM**, and **CONCENTRATION**, represented by numbers. *Power* is physical stuff, *Charm* is social stuff, and *Concentration* is mental stuff. Easy. They will change a lot over the course of your travels and you'll use them often, so keep a close eye on them. Don't panic too much if they drop below 0 – except where the text says otherwise, all that does is make rolls harder for you. As a reward for reading this introduction before diving in, ignore what it tells you at entry **32**, **53**, or **280** (which one you hit will depend on your first choice) and instead, start with each of these statistics at 3. Well done, you.

There is also a whole range of secondary **QUALITIES** you might pick up… {WAVES}, for example. Qualities are always in {CURLY BRACKETS}. Secondary qualities start afresh each new time you play, so if the book tells you to take a Quality you haven't encountered yet, that Quality starts with a score of 1. Keep track of them, because they can seriously change how events unfold. If there's ever a reference to a bonus awarded by a Quality you don't currently have, you don't get that bonus – maybe try to find and acquire it.

You'll also find physical **OBJECTS** you can take with you, and they're always marked in [Square Brackets] to show they're special. They might provide bonuses or help with specific situations. Or not. You can have up to five objects at once. After that, to take something new, you must drop (cross off) something you already have. Some objects are used up when you employ them, so can be deleted at that point.

During your adventures, you're going to run into tests, fights, minigames, and puzzles. They're all clearly labeled.

Just follow the instructions at the time. Oh, and there are also some entries with no obvious link leading to them. The clues on how to find them are in the text, mostly. They're worth your while to sniff out.

You can get killed, at least fictionally. Terminal mistakes finish with The end. If that happens, your adventure is over. Chalk it up to experience and try again from the start. There are several quite different routes through the book, so you definitely won't see everything in one play-through anyway.

Lastly, as you progress you'll be given ACHIEVEMENTS after certain groovy choices or results. There's a full list at the end of the book. When you're given an achievement, tick it off the list – these are good for multiple play-throughs. If you're reading this in ebook format, you'll have to keep notes somewhere else.

There are also some SUPER-ACHIEVEMENTS listed at the end of the book for finishing the adventure with certain objects or qualities in your possession.

And that's all there is to it. Now it's time for adventure – turn the page!

1

The park is less tame than you had hoped. Sure, there are elegant pathways snaking between the trees, and the lampposts are spaced so that the lanterns give everything a nice, warm glow. Beyond these ribbons of safety though, the trees are dense, and there are frequent thickets of shrubbery. Even the roar of the city's eternal traffic is muted, this deep into the grounds. It's probably beautiful during the day, a much needed haven away from San José's grind, but right now, as the mist creeps in, it's just eerie.

Your employer must see some unease on your face, because she smiles reassuringly and reaches down to pat your shoulder gently. "There's nothing to worry about."

At six foot seven, with the build of an Olympian, she's a reassuring presence. She's right, no mugger on Earth is going to voluntarily attack She-Hulk. "Thank you, Ms Walters. I'm fine. It's just... atmospheric."

"It certainly is, and please, do call me Jen."

"I will," you promise. Again. You remind yourself it's OK to be slightly rattled that you're walking through a notoriously sketchy murder-park in the middle of the night with a full-on super hero who has hired you as her in-state paralegal and local advisor.

To think you expected this to be a slow week.

You're about to say something more when you hear an unearthly moan from up ahead. It's not pain, not exactly. There's a hollow note to it, but also a horrible edge of glee. You freeze, skin prickling all over. Is the mist thickening?

The moan continues, getting slowly louder and nastier.

She-Hulk glances back at you and nods approvingly. "Good, keep behind me." Her voice is calm and confident, and you feel momentarily better.

"Oooooo," moans the unseen presence, a wail of hunger and malice. "OoooOO. MOO!"

You blink. Swooping down out of the sky, wickedly long fangs gleaming, eyes glowing as vividly red as the lining of its opera cape, is… a cow?

"Don't meet her eyes," Jen says urgently.

The cow lands on her back legs a few feet in front of She-Hulk, front legs raised in front of her chest in a clear karate stance. "Mooooo," she says again, and pulls her mouth into a ghastly parody of a smile. You realize that like her eyes, her fangs are as red as blood.

Jen takes a step forward, dropping into a wrestler's half-crouch. "Bessie," she says, her voice suddenly grim. "You're making a bad mistake."

"Moooo," the vampire beast replies. It sounds defiant.

"Fine," She-Hulk says. She shoots a glance back in your direction. "Any tips for dealing with an evil vampire farm animal?"

This has to be a dream, you think with sudden relief. Everything's *fine*. Of course you're not in a midnight park with She-Hulk being asked how to deal with undead cows. That would be insane. You're just in bed. Too much cheese, probably. You smile, and decide what to reply.

If this is your first time playing an adventure gamebook, you don't read the numbered entries in numerical order.

Instead, at the end of each entry, you pick an option and turn to that number in the book. Time to try it…

"Try punching the undead horror?" Turn to entry **53**.

"Can you reason with her?" Turn to entry **32**.

"Does she have any weaknesses?" Turn to entry **280**.

2

If you're reading this because you finished the first section and kept right on going, we must warn you that you're going to get confused and bored very quickly. This book really only makes sense if you hop from entry to entry according to the directions. You do you, but we recommend that you go back and decide how to approach Bessie.

Here because you dodged a grab? Great, good to have you. Make a note of the number 98. Thanks!

Jen sways back as the huge man grabs at her, and kicks him in the chest. He leaps as she does, twisting to impact the wall across the street feet first. He then springs off it somehow, cheering wildly, and jumps back to land on a hotel balcony several floors up.

"Kangaroo, of all idiots," she mutters. "This is so undignified." She jumps, sailing up toward Kangaroo's position as he hops over his balcony and falls.

Make an aerial maneuvers test. Roll two dice, add your **POWER** and **CONCENTRATION**, and subtract your {FLAT-FOOTED}, if any.

The total is 15 or more: turn to **135**.

14 or less: turn to **9**.

3

The dining room is surprisingly modernist. There's a bar area just to your left. A dozen simple bench-like wooden tables each offer seating for four. The brown carpet and extensive pot-plants give a subtle feeling of natural space. It looks charming, in a high-end way.

A tall, bald, dark-skinned man is standing between the tables. He's wearing leather trousers and nothing else, showing off an impressive physique. He carries a flaming torch in one hand and a dark ball in the other. Jen snatches something off the bar and is suddenly leaping through the air.

Make a surprise attack test. Roll one die and add your **POWER**.

Total is 7 or more: Before the man can even blink, she is sitting on his chest.

6 or less: The man belches flame as she lands on him, knocking him over. She pins him down, swatting irritably at the small fire in her hair. It smells dreadful. Take **-1 CHARM** and **+1 {INTENSITY}**.

Jen grabs a big jug of water from the bar. She pours it over the man's torch and face in equal measure. "Sorry, Tomás," she says. "I can't risk you burning Ruby's house down."

His angry struggles have absolutely no effect. He says something furious in Spanish as she pulls a cloth off a table, rips it up, then gags and hogties him as easily as if she was changing a toddler.

She pats him on the cheek before standing up. "There, there." He shoots her a look of pure humiliation.

Jen turns to you. "You're doing well so far. Where next? The parlor or the spa?"

"The parlor." Turn to **292**.

"The spa." Turn to **137**.

4

"Keep your head down," Jen says. She's grinning, and limbering up her shoulders. You nod, close your eyes, and pull your jacket up over your face. The smashing starts, and with the extra feedback from the speaker system, it sounds like a Greek god cutting loose on all the plates in the world. Shards smack into your jacket repeatedly, as well as other places, but fortunately Jen is being careful, and you don't take any damage.

But how long does this take? Make a clobbering test. Roll one die and add your **POWER**. If the total is 10 or less, take **+1 {WATCHED}**.

Eventually, silence falls, and you look out to see the floor is ankle-deep in broken glass. The walls are concrete though, and there are three doors onwards. One shows a flower, one a painting, and one a statue.

For the flower door, turn to **255**.

For the painting door, turn to **264**.

For the statue door, turn to **175**.

5

You catch up with Steve, Marion's ex, at the car salesroom where he works. You spot him easily – he's the one who glances over, sees the two of you, and instead of just staring openly like everyone else, he shoves his customer away, and takes off at a dead sprint. Jen ducks back out the front door and leaps easily onto the roof. Ten seconds later, you hear a loud scream, and thirty seconds after that, she comes back round to the front of the building, Steve tucked under one arm.

Take **+1 {WAVES}**.

"Repeat all that," she says.

"It was some huge Aussie thug! He said he was an old friend of Marion's, and he just wanted to surprise her. He didn't even pay me the $500. That's all, I swear!"

She-Hulk jumps again, forty feet straight feet up. Steve is still wailing in terror as she lands, absorbing the impact smoothly in her legs.

Make an intimidation test. Roll one die and add your **POWER**.

8 or more: turn to **57**.

7 or less: turn to **95**.

6

She-Hulk and Chtylok collide in mid-air. The beast must weigh several tons, but She-Hulk's leap has so much force behind it that as the two impact, they drop to the sand together. She's swinging savage punches at the beast as they land, but it completely ignores them to grab her by the head and fling her straight into the stone arena wall as if she was a rag-doll.

She groans and slides down to the sand, but she's already rolling painfully away. A moment later, Chtylok slams a huge fist down, clipping her side. She-Hulk sways aside as she pulls herself to her feet, grabs a hoofed leg, and tries to wrench it. With another shattering "Kraw!", the beast aims a brutal peck at her head.

This is a fierce fight.

Round one: roll two dice, add your **POWER**, and subtract your {**WOBBLY**}. If the total is 14 or more, you win the first round.

Round two: roll two dice, add your **POWER**, and subtract your {**WOBBLY**}. If the total is 14 or more, you win the second round.

If you won both rounds, turn to **245**.

If you lost either round, turn to **108**.

7

She-Hulk circles the robot for a moment, looking a bit winded. It lashes out with its sword, then spins to target you with the gun-nozzles that sprout out of its shoulders. There's a burst of gunfire and... nothing.

ACHIEVEMENT: *Falling at the First Hurdle.*

The end.

8

Arcade sighs dramatically. "So *violent*." Jen growls menacingly, and he shrinks back into his big chair. "Okay, okay," he says quickly. "You win. Don't kill me."

Over the next couple of hours, Arcade is carted away by the police, and the surviving tech gurus and privacy campaigners have been taken to nearby hospitals for emergency treatment, trauma counseling, and/or medical examination, as appropriate. Arcade cheerfully admits he designed this Murderworld to break them and leave them pliable, but even so, the final VIP death toll is eleven.

Ruby comes over to take a look at Arcade's computer systems, and confirms that he did not manage to assemble all the code he required. "You were just in time," she says. "He was still trying to pry vital modules out of Tekeli and Omni."

"What about you, Ruby?" She-Hulk asks, keeping her voice carefully neutral.

She snorts. "Oh, I was tempted. I could unify the six

of us without even breaking a guideline, let alone the law. But you'd be there. Or Thor would, or Spider-Man, or Reed Richards, or Doom, or Kingpin, or... Anyone, really. I don't want to rule the world, Jen. I really don't. Far, *far* too much bother. I'll just keep on being fabulously rich and successful and having a wonderful time. Which reminds me: I'm having a little welcome home bash in a couple of weeks, just a few hundred friends – celebrities and politicians, sure, but also a bunch of anti-corruption activists and other morally upstanding types. Decency is good for business. I really would be delighted if you came. Both of you."

"You never know," Jen says with a smile.

ACHIEVEMENT: *Clean Sweep.*

Final score: 4 stars.

The end.

9

She-Hulk and Kangaroo collide in mid-air. While the big Australian has the body mass, his momentum is no match for the power behind Jen's leap. The pair of them land in a tangled heap on a second-floor balcony, quickly rolling apart.

Kangaroo flails and springs to his feet – right into She-Hulk's foot.

Make a kick test. Roll one die, add your **POWER**, and subtract your {FLAT-FOOTED}, if any.

9 or more: turn to **111**.

8 or less: turn to **72**.

10

The walk round the back of the mansion is tense but uneventful. In the grounds behind the house, you can see extensive grass lawns leading to a huge hedge maze – a preposterous waste of water. The doors Ruby told you about are sliding glass panels, and open into a bright, airy pantry so that delivery people don't have to step one muddy foot further into the building than necessary.

An absolutely gigantic dark-haired woman is standing at the far end of the pantry. She's wearing a purple dress and what must be several pounds of gold chains, rings, bracelets, brooches, and other expensive-looking items of jewelry. Most of the visible stones look like rubies. "She-Hulk," growls the woman. "Glad you came my way."

"Hello, *Teena*," She-Hulk says perfectly calmly. "Where's the Ringmaster?"

Teena just chuckles nastily.

Jen sighs and looks at you. "How shall we do this?"

"Intimidation." Turn to **58**.

"Persuasion." Turn to **148**.

"Reason." Turn to **157**.

11

If you have a white ball, logic says that your bag is not the bag with two black balls. You've pulled out a white ball, so either your bag contains a white ball or a black ball. However, if you have the "black and white" bag, you only end up in this version of reality 50% of the time, but if you have the "two whites" bag, you end up here 100% of the time. That means it's twice as likely that you're currently holding the "two whites" bag than the "black and white" bag – and so the actual probability of getting a second white ball is two-thirds. Congratulations!

Take **+1 {PUZZLER}** and the ACHIEVEMENT: *Improbable*.

Jen grins. "Improbable is nothing. Call me when we're up to impossible."

"Call you what?" you ask.

"You know what to call me."

There's an approving ping from beneath the statue. A section of the terracotta wall shifts color to reveal a pair of doors onwards. They have plaques this time. One says *Temple*, the other *Pool*.

For the temple, turn to **166**.

For the pool, turn to **62**.

12

The reading room is cozy, with comfortable-looking office chairs around a big central study table as well as a couple of big armchairs. The table contains a large scattering of books on robotics, some of them open. From the looks of it, someone has been investigating really huge robots and the materials you'd need to use to construct them. She-Hulk looks at them, then rolls hers eyes and glares in a direction you can't make sense of.

Take +1 {TROUBLESOME}.

"Darn right I'm troublesome," she mutters.

You could settle down in here for a deep-dive into the robotics industry, but you decide to press on.

For the main library, turn to **127**.

For the exit, turn to **206**.

13

Yes, this is a secret entry. Very well done!

ACHIEVEMENT: *Secret One.*

In the corner of Bright's bathroom, under a facecloth, you find a laminated VIP pass for a technology and gaming convention taking place in Los Angeles this weekend, ElectroCon. It doesn't need an inventory spot, so set {EXPO PASS} to 1. While you're at it, take +2 CONCENTRATION for your impressive observation skills.

Now head on up to the attic by turning to **214**.

14

She-Hulk nods, her expression one of firm resolve. It takes her less than two seconds to sink her fingers into the steel security door, rip it out of the doorway, and toss it back into the meadow. You almost want to burst into applause, but instead you follow her inside.

The barn is a big, open-plan office. You're in the entry area, which includes couches, plants, and a reception desk, but beyond that you can see a maze of high-tech workstations, dozens of them, comfortably slotted amid snack machines, foosball tables, beanbags, arcade machines, and other tech toys. There are some doors at the far end.

A pack of people stand between you and the work floor, forty or more of them. Their faces are completely expressionless, and they're clutching improvised weapons – chunks of heavy-looking metal pipe, mostly.

Take +1 {REASONABLE DOUBT}.

An intercom crackles. "Intruders are not one," a male voice says. "They do not make sense."

Instantly the pack are snarling with identical expressions of rage, and as She-Hulk pushes you back, they sprint at you. This is a tricky fight, because She-Hulk has to both keep you safe and avoid permanently harming your attackers. If you have an [Evil Cowbell], ringing it loudly now will help disorient the mob.

Round one: roll two dice and add your POWER and, if you have any, your {TRANSFORMED}. If the total is 13 or more – or you use the [Evil Cowbell] – you win the first round.

Round two: roll two dice and add your POWER and, if you have any, your {TRANSFORMED}. If the total is 12 or more – or you use the [Evil Cowbell] – you win the second round.

If you won both rounds, turn to **145**.

If you lost any rounds, turn to **101**.

15

The abomination lifts She-Hulk off the floor and keeps squeezing. She screams again, this time in pain. It doesn't look good.

Do you have a [Broken Drone] and a [Remote Control]? The drone can't fly, but with the remote, you can get the rotor arms thrashing around wildly. You pitch the drone into the mass, and activate it. Jen tumbles free. Turn to **267**.

Otherwise, make a structural integrity test. Roll one die and add your Power.

11 or more: Jen breaks free. Turn to **267**.

10 or less: she stays wrapped. Turn to **121**.

16

It may seem counter-intuitive, but zero is indeed an even number. The definition of an even number is that it is a multiple of 2, and 2*0 = 0. To put it another way, two even numbers always add to an even number, and one odd and one even number always add to an odd number. 1+0=1, which is odd; 2+0=2, which is even. Well done!

Take **+1 {PUZZLER}** and **+2 CONCENTRATION**.

Three doors become visible in the grey mists. One shows a flower, one a painting, the third a statue.

For the flower door, turn to **255**.

For the painting door, turn to **264**.

For the statue door, turn to **175**.

17

You have to go through some odd, semi-deserted back rooms to get to the VIP area's staff entrance, but although it all feels weirdly liminal, no one challenges you. It's a simple wooden door, with a prominent card reader next to it. There are no guards, but there is a tired-looking woman in a cheap suit leaning against the wall nearby, clearly snatching a moment of peace and quiet.

"We don't know what's inside so I don't want to just punch through," Jen mutters. "But we could try asking the lady for help, or I could have a go at bypassing the card reader. Any preferences?"

"Let's ask for help." Turn to **262**.

"Let's MacGyver the reader." Turn to **165**.

"Let's try the main entrance." Turn to **75**.

18

Pacific Bay is a lovely little town on the California coast, north of San Francisco. It's a pleasant afternoon when you get there, and the sun gives the pale buildings and their dark roofs a little extra charm. The downtown strip is quiet, and a few stores are shuttered. They're a curious mix of low and high end, an aging tool and home improvements store nestled between a gourmet French restaurant and an exquisite little wine bar, while over the road a Vanguard flagship store completely overshadows a sprawling bodega advertising cheap frozen chicken.

You pass through the town and head out to the compound, which is only a half-mile out. You can't see a thing from the outside, just very tall white walls, thick-looking gates also painted white, and a few big renditions of the company's spiky V-logo. There was a gatehouse outside the gates – the ground still bears the marks – but it's been dismantled, and there isn't even a visible intercom.

"I could just jump us over the wall," She-Hulk says. "It might trigger some alarms, but it's an option."

If you have {DELIVERY PATTERNS} of 1, you can try intercepting groceries by turning to **273**.

If you have {FOOD TRUCK} of 1 and want to try talking your way onto a sandwich van, turn to **97**.

If you want to search the area around the compound, turn to **65**.

Or to scale the wall, turn to **119**.

19

You tap at the keyboard for a while, but nothing happens. The correct answer to the puzzle is actually *117* – calculate terms in brackets first, then calculate multiplications and divisions, and only then calculate additions and subtractions.

"It was worth a shot," Jen says, and presses the intercom button with a faint shrug.

"Yes?" The voice crackling through the speaker is brisk and female, businesslike.

"Jennifer Walters, attorney-at-law. May I speak with someone in charge?"

There's a long silence. "It's your funeral," the voice says finally. "I'm upstairs, if you make it."

How... encouraging.

"Thank you, ma'am," Jen says. "We'll be there shortly."

"We'll see." The door buzzes, and you enter a corridor with polished wooden floors and off-white walls, decorated sparsely with paintings of futuristic cityscapes. It all looks suspiciously normal. There are simple wooden doors at each end of the corridor with nothing much to distinguish them, except that there's a faint draft of fresh air coming from the door to the right. She-Hulk looks at you expectantly.

"Let's go left." Turn to **127**.

"Let's go right." Turn to **206**.

20

The abomination is many times larger than She-Hulk, but so far, it's been unable to get a solid hold on her. On the other hand, her blows seem to be having no impact on it. Even when she rips a pseudopod off, it just dissolves out of her grasp and then flows back to the main mass. Although neither side is making any headway, the battle is frantic.

You might be able to help with a well-timed strategic suggestion?

"Go for the eye!" Turn to **69**.

"Attack from inside it!" Turn to **267**.

"Let it grab you!" Turn to **219**.

21

If anyone at Tekeli takes exception to your grimly dogged, slime-drenched exit, they keep it very much to themselves. That evening, repeatedly showered and freshly clothed, you head over to meet Ruby in the restaurant of the Ever-Grande Hotel in the SoFA district. The area bills itself as the city's artistic hub. It's certainly an eclectic mix of architectural styles.

The Ever-Grande is a stylish older building that makes you think of hotels from Hollywood's golden period. It has a tall, elegant lobby that leans heavily toward pale stone, red carpets, and gilded metal. A huge chandelier lights the space, and the guests are split evenly between expensive business-wear and even more expensive, carefully distressed outfits that do their best to scream the wearer's creative genius.

You've been in there about fifteen seconds, just long enough for the whispers and nudging to start, when the front door explodes behind you. The place erupts into screams and chaos, as you and Jen spin round. Take +1 {WAVES}.

A huge, brass-colored wheel has rammed through the front of the hotel. It's about seven feet in diameter, with a tread three feet wide, and there's a minimalist cockpit mounted on gyroscopes in the middle. It looks like someone obsessed with monster trucks fused a hamster wheel with a Segway. Hefty multi-barreled alien devices that could be chain guns sit either side of the cockpit, and bigger tubes in the same style that might be rocket launchers are attached to other parts of the frame. A man is sitting in the cockpit, dressed in green body armor and wearing a squared-off motorbike helmet the same color as the wheel. You can see his face through the two-tone visor.

"Really?" Jen says, her voice heavy with disapproval. "Big Wheel? He's not even the original."

There's a loud whine, and then he's zipping backwards out into the road, pulling more of the hotel down as he goes. Something blurs in front of you, and then a different man is standing in the rubble. He's dressed in a bright red jumpsuit with a golden starburst, and some sort of futuristic space helmet, and he's tossing a fireball from hand to hand.

"None may stand before the might of Oort, the Living Comet!" declares the man. "Not even the She-Hulk!"

Ruby strides up out of the panicking crowd to stand

beside Jen. She has dropped her disguise, and her red pantsuit is colored to match her head precisely. Several long tentacles snake out of it, waving lazily. They end in nasty-looking spiked lumps. As Oort goggles at her, She-Hulk grabs a chunk of debris and flings it at him so quickly it actually whistles through the air. The masonry takes him in the front of the helmet, and he's flung back out into the road.

"Time to dance," Ruby says. "Where do you want me?"

Jen darts a questioning glance back at you. She's definitely taking this whole extended interview concept a bit far, but she'd overrule a bad mistake, right?

"You have no idea," she mutters.

Ignoring that, you take a breath, and decide…

"Offence." Turn to **248**.

"Defence." Turn to **56**.

22

"KHAAAW!!" With a howl of fury, Chtylok goes absolutely berserk. You cower in terror as it thrashes around in a wild frenzy. She-Hulk and the Thing take cover across the arena, battered and exhausted. It lashes out at the arena itself, bringing whole sections crashing down. You watch in horror as the ceiling cracks above you. The last thing you see is a huge piece of masonry plummeting down toward you. Oh no.

ACHIEVEMENT: *So Near And Yet So Far.*

The end.

23

A young man in a pale grey t-shirt and blue jeans is sitting at a table on his own, staring at a mug of coffee. The oversized surveillance camera watches you join him. Take +1 {COOL}.

"But which sense of 'cool?'" Jen murmurs. "That's the rub."

The man looks up, nods, and looks down again.

"Hello," Jen says.

The man nods again.

"How's the coffee?"

"Wonderful," the man says calmly.

"Right. And what do you do here?"

"Here I drink coffee."

Jen's smile slips a little. "I meant, what do you do at Omni and Grey?"

"Here I drink coffee. We are one. It makes sense."

"I … see. Thanks. Enjoy your coffee."

"It's wonderful."

"Bye."

The man nods yet again, and the pair of you walk to a quiet spot.

"I don't think there's any point bothering these poor people any further," Jen says. "Where now?"

To visit the lodge, if you haven't already, turn to **152**.

To head out the back of the café and go exploring, turn to **223**.

24

It takes about ten minutes, but eventually a nervous-looking young woman comes to escort you to Gould's office. She leaves you at the door. He turns out to be a very tall man, middle aged, with shrewd eyes. He ushers you politely into his expensively large office, orders some coffee, and the meeting starts. It's immediately clear that he has absolutely no idea what this meeting is about, but he's damned if he's going to let on. So what follows is the most peculiar verbal dance you've ever witnessed as he and Jen exchange a series of allusions, bland nothings, and vaguely portentous statements.

Gould is absorbed in the conversation, and his black pass-card is on his desk. If you're very careful, you might be able to swipe it while he's particularly distracted. Make a sleight of hand check. Roll one die and add your **CONCENTRATION**. If the total is 10 or more, you may add the **[Onyx Pass-card]** to your inventory if you wish.

Ten more nervous minutes pass before Jen stands up, signaling the end of the meeting.

Gould looks thoughtful. "You've given me a lot to think about, Ms Walters," he says. "After this weekend, we should facilitate further consideration."

"Absolutely," she says. "Until then."

The pair of you leave, and she sighs. "That was ridiculous. He's completely clueless. He didn't even realize that when I said 'Swiss livestock', I was talking about Bessie. No wonder he's scared of Ruby."

You head back downstairs, to where the restricted section beckons. "I think we might need to make our own entrance," Jen says.

If you have the [Onyx Pass-card], turn to **126**.

To see what Jen has in mind, turn to **131**.

25

Maybe "home office" was optimistic. The room is packed full of computer equipment, but it's for gaming, not work. The seat looks ripped from a racecar, and there are three huge monitors and several computers. Almost everything sports rainbow-colored LEDs.

This room actually looks lived in, though, so he did come home occasionally, at least. That's something.

You scan the bookshelf while She-Hulk checks the main desk. It's mostly comic-books – cool, but not what you need. Then you hear a tiny click followed by a thin swishing noise, and look round to see a sword on a spring-loaded arm slashing straight at Jen's head.

Take +1 {REASONABLE DOUBT} and +1 {MICROSWITCHED} and make a trap! test. Roll one die.

4 or more: She calmly slides aside and snatches the sword off the arm. If you want a [Sword], you may take it.

3 or less: She swats the sword away like shooing a fly. It breaks into a half-dozen pieces.

She looks at the metal arm. "These traps are certainly enthusiastic, but they're not very good. Interesting. Where next?"

To head to the dining room, turn to **52**.

To go to the lounge, turn to **147**.

To make your way upstairs, turn to **261**.

26

The door with the washbasin opens onto a light, airy tiled room that contains a wealth of lush pot-plants, several automatic massage chairs, a row of sinks with washbasins, and a stack of facecloths. The air is lightly lemon-scented, and there is some quietly relaxing music tinkling in the background. Opposite the door you came in by, there's another door with a sign saying *Arena: Combatants Only*.

"Hmm," Jen says. "This feels like those stockpiles of ammo and health kits you find right before the boss fight."

"So it's not another trap?"

She shrugs. "There are traps and there are traps. But we can use the facilities if you like." If you freshen up and get a quick massage, make a note that you did so.

"Are we ready to see what joys the Arena has for us?" she asks.

"Sure." Turn to **197**.

"Let's check the coffee-cup room first." Turn to **299**.

27

The gala room is big and bright, lots of wood-floored space bordered by large circular tables that bear heavy white linen tablecloths. The near wall is heavily mirrored, while the far wall is made of tall windows separated by thin wooden strips. It's all very light and spacious.

As you enter, a pair of tall, athletic men in extremely tight lilac bodysuits are flipping from opposite corners of the main floor toward the center. They land next to each other with identical flourishes, identical nasty grins, and identical faces. They have thin little mustaches that barely look worth the effort. Each extends a hand, as if expecting applause.

"Hey there," Jen says, her voice flat.

They spring into action again, bouncing and flipping across the room. Maybe they're going for misdirection, but they're steadily getting closer. There is a moment to spare. Jen looks at you questioningly.

To suggest meeting them on the ground, turn to **297**.

To suggest meeting them in the air, turn to **187**.

28

You take a step toward the portal. She-Hulk places a hand on your shoulder. "I'm not going to tell you what to do, but if you go through that portal, everything will change. I won't be able to come with you, and I won't be able help you any more. So please, just be sure that this is what you want."

If you still want to go ahead, turn to **220**.

To stay in this reality, explore the lab by turning to **184**.

29

The odd one out is 67. Depending on where you came from, that's either because it's not the square or the cube of another number (the kitchens), because it is a prime number (the snack bar), or because it is not a multiple of 17 (the guest suite.)

Take **-1 CONCENTRATION** and **+1 {INTENSITY}** and turn to **67**.

30

"I'm not sure why the judge refused me bail," Ruby says. "I'm too deeply invested in Silicon Valley to be a flight risk. But anyway, I was going to be late for meeting Tony Bright, and he was apparently early. I have time-stamped video recordings on my computer at home from an online meeting I had to take. The police have flatly refused to go look. If you take those to the judge, it'll be clear I was elsewhere at the time of the murder. That should do it."

She-Hulk nods. "Where's home?"

"I have a mansion in the hills near San Gregorio."

Of *course* she does.

"Lovely," Jen says. "Any surprises waiting there?"

"Not on my account. But the butler did tell me that the staff had all been chased out by, and I quote, 'crazy thugs.'

She didn't hang around to get names or anything. So I imagine there's someone there."

"Wonderful."

For more details about the mansion itself, turn to **114**.
To head over there, turn to **209**.

31

The judge's sister is as easy to find as following the trail that Kangaroo has left through the dust blanketing the place. She's on the top floor of the hotel, in a run-down room that might have been impressive eighty years ago. She's being watched by a wiry old man with a white handlebar mustache. He's standing in front of the large open window, dressed completely in black, with a hood that exposes only his face and chin. As you enter, he nods to himself.

"We're here for Marion," She-Hulk says firmly.

"But of course you are, my dear," the old man says. He has a crisp English accent. "I have absolutely no intention of attempting to impede you."

"That makes a change."

He smiles ruefully. "One must know when to cut one's losses."

"I have some questions."

"Undoubtedly. I, alas, do not have the answers – all I can tell you is that our principal is in Los Angeles, that he has a lot of money invested in whatever scheme this is part of, and that he has quite the thin skin regarding criticism of his self-assumed artistic flair. Oh, and that I, of course, am the Black Fox." He pauses, then bows in a sweepingly elegant fashion. "It has been a delight to make your acquaintance, Ms Walters. I wish you every possible luck in your endeavors."

He hops backwards, onto the window sill, then steps back again and vanishes. You dart to the window to see him swinging across the street on a line fastened to a billboard on another building. He vanishes through an open window across the way, waving in your direction as the darkness swallows him up.

"There's no point chasing him. He'll have an entire escape route already set up," Jen says. "His kind always do. But I've heard of him. He's a superb jewel thief – world class. An expensive choice to babysit a kidnap victim. Interesting. So, what now?"

To get Marion back to the judge, turn to **182**.

To interview Marion first, turn to **118**.

To call Ruby and fill her in, turn to **188**.

32

Before we proceed with the adventure, let's set up the stats for your team of She-Hulk and the Paralegal. There are three core scores: **POWER**, **CHARM**, and **CONCENTRATION**. You remember that from the introduction, which you absolutely read. Right? Hm.

Power represents She-Hulk's current strength, agility and resilience. Very helpful for punching things, which is definitely a talent of She-Hulk's, as well as throwing things, leaping over things, breaking things, and all sorts of other tasks you'll encounter in time.

Charm is a measure of how eloquent and persuasive other people consider She-Hulk to be at the time. It rises and falls with her patience level, and it can be affected by physical effects and events that might impact other people's perceptions. Being covered head to toe in reeking ectoplasmic goo is bad for your **CHARM**, for example.

Concentration, lastly, indicates your team's current level of mental ability. It's handy for solving problems, spotting objects that are out of the way or hard to notice, and thinking up clever solutions on the fly. You'll still have to solve the puzzles in this book on your own, however.

Your core stats will change repeatedly over the course of your adventure, so you'll need to keep track of them on a piece of paper or something. You start with **POWER** of 2, **CHARM** of 3, and **CONCENTRATION** of 2.

Right. Back to the game.

• • •

Grinning like a crazy person, you suggest, "Can you reason with her?"

"Maybe." She-Hulk shrugs. "Bessie is a four hundred and fifty year-old vampire, though. Even human vampires don't last that long unless they're incredibly strong-willed." She turns to the cow. "You know how strong I am, Hellcow. There's no need to do this. I don't want to hurt you. Just float away."

"Moooo."

"That's certainly intriguing, but even so, I urge you to reconsider," Jen says. "There are always more clients."

"Moo." Bessie flickers forward, faster than the eye can follow, just a smear of black and brown against the night. Then she's right up in She-Hulk's face, those glittering red eyes boring into Jen's. "Mooooooooo," she says, suddenly quiet and weirdly suggestive.

Make a willpower test. Roll one die, and add your **CHARM** and **CONCENTRATION** to it. What's the result?

Total is 7 or more: turn to **173**.

6 or less: turn to **86**.

33

The mailbox door leads to an old-fashioned wood-paneled dining room. There's a big, heavy dining table covered with a white tablecloth, and a long sideboard holds supplies of cutlery, plates, napkins, and other dining things. A panel shoots up in the wall, and a large pack of ferocious dogs bursts into the room, growling and snarling.

This is a tricky fight.

Round one: roll two dice and add your **POWER**. If the total is 15 or more, or you have and want to use up [Illegal Pepper Spray], you win the first round.

Round two: roll two dice and add your **POWER**. If the total is 13 or more, you win the second round.

If you lost either round, you get a distractingly painful bite. Take **-1 CONCENTRATION**.

Once Jen has scared the dogs into fleeing, you see a couple of exits, one marked with a triangle, and one with a circle.

For the triangle door, turn to **46**.

For the circle door, turn to **215**.

34

The Thing shakes his head. "Naw. I haven't even been inside the center yet. I heard a couple of staff talking about 'the red VIP zone', but that's all I got. Sorry."

To ask if he's seen anything suspicious, turn to **270**.

To head in to the Expo, turn to **230**.

35

You head over to a table where a plaid-shirted young woman is picking at a large, delicious-looking croissant, and sit down. A chunky surveillance cam watches you. Take +1 {COOL}.

The woman looks up and smiles. "Hi. You're green."

"Hi," Jen says. "Yes, I am."

"That's nice," the woman says. "It's a calm color."

Jen blinks. "That's new. What's it like here?"

"Wonderful! We are one. Everything is just perfect and lovely and normal."

"Uh, that's great."

"Isn't it?"

"Yes. Yes it is. Do you know Anthony Bright?"

The woman's brow furrows for just one instant. "I don't think so. Do I?"

Jen pats her hand reassuringly. "No, I'm sure you don't. Everything is fine."

"Wonderful!"

"You have a lovely day," Jen says, standing up.

"Oh! I will," promises the woman.

The two of you retreat a short distance. "That was weird," you say. Take +1 {REASONABLE DOUBT}.

She-Hulk nods. "Definitely. So what now?"

"Let's risk a coffee." Turn to **90**.

"Let's try another person." Turn to **23**.

36

Bi-Beast flings She-Hulk to the floor and stamps on her chest savagely. You hear bones splintering, and she shrieks in agony. "Jen!" you scream.

The android looks up at you with an expression of mild curiosity on its faces. It reaches out, pulls a chunk out of a column, and hurls it at you like a missile. You don't even have time to flinch.

ACHIEVEMENT: *It's Doric Time.*

The end.

37

Rb. The chemical symbol for Rubidium, the element with the atomic number of 37. Very, very nice work. Definitely pat yourself on the back for spotting that clue.

Looking behind the chalk-board, which is free-standing, you see a [Glowing Pearl]. There's something oddly fascinating about the way about the way its glow subtly shifts and dapples. If you choose to take it, the pearl increases your CHARM by 2 for as long as it is in your inventory.

ACHIEVEMENT: *Secret Four.*

Now turn back to the laboratory at **184**.

38

You make use of the utilitarian restrooms, tidy up a little, and generally get yourselves together. Jen is, it has to be said, rather intimidatingly together already, but no harm done.

Take **+1 CHARM** and **+1 CONCENTRATION**.
  To go wait for Ruby, turn to **59**.
  To ask the staff about her, turn to **123**.

39

You pass from the sterile corridor to a large room, also dazzlingly white, and brighter than the corridor was. One wall of the room is glass, but the space beyond is completely dark. There are several machines in here that look like they were stolen from the set of a retro-futuristic sci-fi movie. They are complicated, inscrutable, and rather off-putting.

On the wall opposite the window, there's an extensive control panel colored an upsettingly 1972-vintage shade of bright orange with lime highlights and brown trim. A door on the far side of the room leads onwards.

"This reminds me of one of Doom's lairs," She-Hulk says. "You're not missing anything, I promise."

  If you'd like to investigate the control panel, turn to **45**.
  To study the glass panel, turn to **225**.
  Or leave the room by turning to **206**.

40

With Oort unconscious and Big Wheel's wheel melted down to scrap by Ruby's energy beams, things gradually begin to calm down. It's another hour before the villains are safely in the custody of the authorities. Miraculously, no one was seriously hurt, and Ruby and Jen are completely unscathed. Take +1 {SIMPATICO} and the ACHIEVEMENT: *Teamwork*.

The three of you retreat down the street to a café with a private room that opens near-magically to Ruby's ebony credit card. Take +1 POWER and +1 CONCENTRATION.

"Tell me about Tekeli," Ruby says.

"Pattern recognition systems built using alien tissue," Jen says. "I have footage." She shows Ruby the clip she took of the space lab computer systems.

"That's it," Ruby says unhappily. "Total global information control."

"It's got to be stopped," Jen says.

"I was supposed to be in jail this weekend, but everyone else load-bearing in the six companies is going to be at ElectroCon LA. Whoever is behind this, he thinks that by the end of the Expo, he'll have everything he needs."

"Then that's where we have to be."

"I'm not the frontal assault type. I'm going to drop into the background. I prefer working behind the scenes anyway."

Jen nods. "That makes sense."

To ask what Ruby means by "load-bearing" people, turn to **158**.

To ask about total information control, turn to **172**.

41

We're afraid that although it may seem counter-intuitive, but zero is an even number, mathematically. The definition of an even number is that it is a multiple of 2, and $2*0 = 0$. To put it another way, two even numbers and two odd numbers always add to an even number, and one odd and one even number always add to an odd number. $1+0=1$, which is odd; $2+0=2$, which is even.

Take **-1 CONCENTRATION**.

Three doors become visible in the grey mists. One shows a flower, one a painting, the third a statue.

For the flower door, turn to **255**.

For the painting door, turn to **264**.

For the statue door, turn to **175**.

42

The concrete path is reasonably short and straight, at least for this place. Without much fuss, it leads you to a humming electrical substation surrounded by a chain-link fence.

"That probably supplies primary power to this whole complex," She-Hulk says. "Although there will certainly be backup generators." You nod. "It looks fragile," she adds. Perhaps it does, to her.

If you ask She-Hulk to destroy the generator, set your {**TRANSFORMED**} to 1, and make a finesse test. Roll one die, and add your **CONCENTRATION** to it. If the total is 6 or less, there's a huge shower of sparks that burn holes in Jen's

suit, and set some of the undergrowth smoldering. Take
-1 CHARM, **+1 {BURNING}**, and **+1 {WAVES}**.

There's nothing else here, so you have to retract your steps.

To try the grass track, turn to **61**.

To follow the pleasant walkway, turn to **164**.

43

The big double doors to the guest suite are secured with a keypad that opens to the same code you used on the gate. You go through to a large, inviting lounge area that reminds you of photos you've seen of ski chalets – lots of pine, comfortable rugs, soft-looking couches, and what looks like a well-stocked bar. It's a bit unusual, but then so is California.

A wiry-looking young man springs up out of a couch. He's in a ridiculous blue and pink get-up – it even has flared gauntlets and booties – and a crested mask that really only covers his scalp and cheek bones. If he's trying to hide his identity, he's failing. He can't be more than nineteen. He and Jen stare at each other for a moment.

"You're not the Swordsman," she says.

He looks a bit hurt at that. "En garde!"

She shakes her head. "No."

"En garde!" he repeats, sounding angry. Jen just shakes her head wearily. The man leaps over the couch, flourishing a shiny broadsword, and lunges ferociously at her. The blow takes her over the heart. It doesn't even dent her skin. She reaches up, plucks the sword away, and idly ties it into a knot. The young man bursts into tears, then dashes past you and out the building.

Jen sighs. "Epic, as always. Where next? The library's straight ahead, and the gala room is to the left."

"Let's try the library." Turn to **64**.

"How about the gala room?" Turn to **27**.

44

The back yard is every bit as lovely and sterile as the front. You had half-expected more personality back here, out of sight, but no. Most of the curtains are closed along the back of the house, but the kitchen door lets you see into a large, expensive domain of glinting chrome and white marble. The door is locked, of course – not that a locked door is going to slow She-Hulk down when she wants in – but there's a pair of cellar doors near the corner of the building that don't have any visible fastening, and the big hinges on this side mean that they open outwards.

"Do you like cellars?" Jen asks pleasantly.

"I love them." Turn to **251**.

"I prefer kitchens." Turn to **156**.

"The front looked more inviting." Turn to **236**.

45

The control panel is currently deactivated. You can see a bunch of small lights built into it, all of them dark for now, and it has a number of dials and switches, but there's no actual information as to what it is supposed to control or why. There's a button labeled "Informatics" and another labeled "Rover" – and neither of them do anything. The only instruction anywhere is next to a big icon that might possibly represent a piece of broccoli, and that says, "Lose three days and decimate." All rather unhelpful.

To study the glass panel, turn to **225**.

To leave the room, turn to **206**.

46

The triangle door leads you into small room with oddly knobbly surfaces, a plinth holding an orb in the center, and an uncomfortable chandelier hanging from the ceiling. It takes a moment, but then you realize that everything around you is made from bones. Human-looking bones. The knobbly walls are made of tightly-packed femurs, the chandelier is designed from ribs and vertebrae and collarbones, and the orb on the plinth is absolutely a human skull.

She-Hulk shakes her head in disgust. "This is not cool."

Red lights flare in the skull's eyes, and panels of bone rise up out of the floor, dividing the ossuary into sections.

This is a maze minigame!

Start at the node in the top left marked *IN*. In each node, follow the directions, rolling a die to decide your exit. When you hit an entry number, turn to that entry.

If you don't like your roll, you may re-roll the die, but only twice in this game.

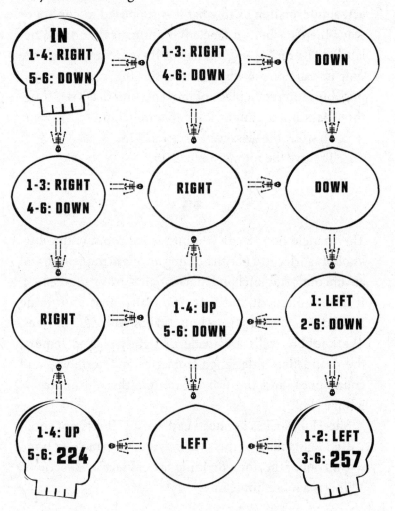

47

You scan your surroundings nervously, but She-Hulk finds a door that leads inside the walls before any further problems assail you. You both enter, and find yourself in a series of empty, possibly decommissioned barracks that lead on to a security station. There's an entire computerized system in here, and it might be possible to blunt the automated defenses a bit.

Make a hacking test. Roll one die and add your **CONCENTRATION**. If the total is 8 or more, take **+1 {DRONED}**.

While She-Hulk is working on hacking the computer, you look around and spot a small **[Remote Control]**. You may take it if you wish.

If you have **{SECURE}** of 1 or more, turn to **109**.

To head into the courtyard, turn to **202**.

If you want to leave the wall up against the main building, turn to **167**.

48

"Jennifer Walters, attorney-at-law with my own practice," she says coolly. "An employee of yours was murdered recently, Mr Winton, one Anthony Bright. We might be able to avoid hauling Omni and Grey in front of the judge if you are prepared to give us information about the deceased."

Make an intimidation test. Roll one die, and add your **POWER** to it. If your total is 7 or more, take **+1 POWER**.

"Of course," Winton says smoothly. "Tony was one of our software engineers, until suddenly he was not. Are you looking for sense? The world can be a senseless place. That's why we exist, you know. We want to help things make sense. This campus is a haven, a place designed to make sense. It's so important to make sense, don't you think? But of course you do, how could it be otherwise. I'm so glad we got the chance to have this little chat. I do understand how busy you are however, so I'll let you get on with it."

"Right." Jen sounds thoughtful. "Thanks."

She turns around, and you follow her out. Off to one side, you note a bulky surveillance cam watching you. Take **+1 {COOL}**.

As soon as you get outside, she stops. "That was curious." Take **+1 {REASONABLE DOUBT}**.

Paths lead off into the woodland behind the visitor's lodge, and there's no one immediately visible to tell you not to wander off. There's also the café, though.

To explore the grounds, turn to **223**.

To try the café if you haven't already, turn to **74**.

Bi-Beast snorts and lunges for She-Hulk, reaching out a massive arm to try to grab her by the head. She rolls to the left, dodging the grab, and mutters something you don't quite catch. It lifts a foot to stamp down on her. She seizes the ankle and heaves, and the android collapses back onto the ground with a crash that makes the floor shake. As it gets up again, she retreats back toward the altar, luring it away from you.

This is a hard fight.

Round one: roll two dice, add your **POWER**, and subtract your {PENALTY}. This round only, if you have an [Experimental Gauntlet], add **+2** as She-Hulk smashes Bi-Beast in the face. If the total is 12 or more, you win the first round.

Round two: roll two dice, add your **POWER**, and subtract your {PENALTY}. This round only, if you have [Spiked Knuckles], add **+2** as She-Hulk tries to blind it. If the total is 13 or more, you win the second round.

Round three: roll two dice, add your **POWER**, and subtract your {PENALTY}. This round only, if you have a [Stained Machete], add **+2** as She-Hulk tries to damage its knee joints. If the total is 12 or more, you win the third round.

If you won two or more rounds, turn to **256**.

If not, turn to **228**.

50

You wait nervously for a moment when no one is looking in your direction, and then follow Jen into the restroom area. Rather than head to the ladies – or, indeed, the gents – she beelines for a maintenance door, and pulls it open with a soft cracking noise. You go through into a long room filled with cleaning and hygiene supplies, and she shuts the door behind you.

"Hmm," she says, looking around. "I was going to wait, but there's another door in the opposite corner. Let's see."

That opens out into the entrance of another set of restrooms, presumably back to back with the ones you entered, and through there into a canteen. It's busy, but for the moment, you're free of observation.

"We could try to follow someone through into the restricted section," Jen says. "Or we could just make our own entrance."

"Let's try to slip in." Turn to **171**.

"Let's be direct." Turn to **131**.

51

She-Hulk patiently bats the flying S-stars away, so they cut into the walls instead. As one hits, there's a loud crackle, a flare of power, and the light coming up from the bathroom dims. A moment later you hear various burglar alarms start to ring off in the distance, as the entire neighborhood's power shorts out. Oops.

Take +1 {WAVES} and -1 POWER, and the ACHIEVEMENT: *Brownout.*

Do you have {AFLAME} of 1 or more? If so, you realize that the fire from the burning cabinet has spread to the house when you see smoke and hints of flame coming through the attic wall. Your only choice at this point is to retreat quickly, write the house off as a bad deal, and try Bright's workplace instead. Turn to **191**.

Spellcheck laughs again, sounding completely demented. You hear a magazine being clicked into place, and duck back a little further. He's got a huge, unwieldy industrial-looking gun-like device now.

"Please put that down before you hurt yourself," Jen says.

"You'd like that!" Spellcheck shouts, and cackles.

"Yes I would!"

"Spike-Gun!" he shrieks.

She-Hulk sighs, and charges him.

This is an easy fight. Roll two dice, add your **POWER**, and subtract your {DELAYED}.

If the total is 7 or more, turn to **129**.

If the total is 6 or less, turn to **179**.

52

The dining room is wide and airy, and dominated by a large, formal table that could easily seat twelve, but only has chairs for eight. Apart from a pristine white tablecloth, it's surprisingly empty. A silver-edged mirror along one wall adds to the light in the room. Next to the door, there's a tall, classical-looking statue of a woman holding a jug of water.

She-Hulk eyes the statue, then cracks her fist down on top of its head. It shatters into plaster fragments. She bends down, searches through the mess for a moment, and stands up holding a broken mechanical device.

"It's a dart trap," she says, showing you a small metal dart from inside the mess. "A cheap one, too. It's all a bit…"

"Unimpressive?" you suggest.

She nods. "Doesn't seem like Ruby's style."

Add +1 {REASONABLE DOUBT}.

Now, to head to the kitchen, turn to **156**.

To go to the lounge, turn to **147**.

To make your way upstairs, turn to **261**.

53

Before we continue with the adventure, let's set up the stats for your team of She-Hulk and the Paralegal. There are three core stats, **POWER**, **CHARM**, and **CONCENTRATION**. You remember that from the introduction, which you absolutely read, yeah? Hm.

Power represents She-Hulk's current strength, agility and resilience. Very helpful for punching things, which will turn out useful any moment now, as well as throwing things, leaping over things, breaking things, and all sorts of other tasks you'll encounter in time.

Charm is a measure of how eloquent and persuasive other people consider She-Hulk to be at the time. It rises and falls with her patience level, and it can be affected by physical effects and events that might impact other people's perceptions. Being covered head to toe in reeking ectoplasmic goo is bad for your **CHARM**, for example.

 Concentration, finally, indicates your team's current level of mental ability. It's handy for solving problems, spotting objects that are out of the way or hard to notice, and thinking up clever solutions on the fly. You'll still have to solve the puzzles in this book on your own, however.

Your core stats will change repeatedly over the course of your adventure, so you'll need to keep track of them on a piece of paper or something. You start with **POWER** of 3, **CHARM** of 2, and **CONCENTRATION** of 2.

Right – back to the game…

Grinning like a crazy person, you suggest, "Try punching the fiend?"

She-Hulk nods. "That's always an option." She glares at Bessie ferociously, and flexes her astonishingly well-developed muscles. "What about it, Hellcow? You've got precisely one chance to run before I smash you into the middle of next week."

"Moo-oo-oo-oo-oo."

You realize with astonishment that the cow is actually laughing. Disdainfully, even.

"Well, I warned you," Jen says.

Bessie flickers forward, faster than the eye can follow, a smear of black and brown against the night. Then she's right up in She-Hulk's face, those glittering red eyes boring into Jen's. "Moooooooooo," she says, suddenly quiet and weirdly suggestive.

Make a willpower test. Roll one die, and add your **CHARM** and **CONCENTRATION** to it. What's the result?.

Total of 7 or more: turn to **173**.

6 or less: turn to **86**.

54

The food court is busy, but there's room to walk around, and the noise isn't completely deafening. It smells unpleasantly of stale oil and mildew, and you resolve not to eat anything here that the staff have cooked. The line for hot food is pretty long anyway.

The vending machines that run along one wall are a bit less packed, probably because they're insanely overpriced. Fifteen bucks for a two-dollar soda is, like, daylight robbery. Still, if you want to swallow your outrage and take **+1 {SHAKEN}**, you may purchase one drink, which you can either drink now or save for later if you have the inventory space. A **[Sports Drink]** will give you **+2 POWER**; a **[Hot Chocolate]** will give you **+2 CHARM**;

or a **[Triple Espresso]** will give you **+2 CONCENTRATION**.

"Byrne provided much better drinks," Jen mutters.

"Like, the rock star?" you ask.

"Who?"

"Never mind," you say.

To try the games hall, turn to **263**.

To try information, turn to **176**.

To wander the complex hoping to spot something, turn to **88**.

55

She-Hulk staggers back from a particularly savage onslaught. She quickly jumps back a couple more feet and braces herself. The Hellcow laughs, the sound low and evil, then explodes into a cloud of fog that sinks into the underlying mist and vanishes.

She-Hulk sighs. "Typical." She looks around warily. "She won't have gone far." An eerie bovine cackle floats out of the night in answer to her statement. "To me! Quick!" She-Hulk yells.

You start forward, feeling a rush of air behind you as you begin running. Somewhere up above, you hear a strangely mangled hiss.

"We need some cover. I'll stay right behind you. Head for that oak tree."

"Right," you say, and walk briskly toward the big tree She-Hulk indicated.

Make an awareness test. Roll one die, and add your **CONCENTRATION** to it.

6 or more: turn to **226**.

5 or less: turn to **268**.

56

"We need you on defense," you say.

"Are you quite certain?" Ruby asks.

Jen shrugs. "Let's try it."

"Fine." She sounds like she'll be having words with you about this later, though. Take **-1 CONCENTRATION**.

For now, she squares off, facing the gap in the lobby wall. A loud whine gives you a moment's warning, and then Big Wheel is crashing back into the building again. This time, he shoots straight through the gap and into the lobby properly, weird chain guns firing. A screen of red force energy spreads in front of the two women, emanating from Ruby's head. The bullets crash into it, seemingly endless. Ruby is forced back a step, and you see her trying to brace her feet.

A blast of shining plasma jets past you, straight toward She-Hulk. Even five feet away, it's horribly hot. You panic for a moment, but she just sways lazily, and it splashes against some stonework. Jen growls, and lunges at Oort, who is now nearby.

Oort is not particularly strong, but he is extremely fast, so this is a tough fight.

Round one: roll two dice, add your **POWER**, and subtract your {LIT UP}, if any. If the total is 14 or more, you win the first round.

Round two: roll two dice, add your **POWER**, and subtract your {LIT UP}, if any. If the total is 13 or more, you win the second round.

If you lost both rounds, take **-3 POWER** in plasma damage. That stuff is *hot*.

If you won both rounds, turn to **122**.

If you lost one or both rounds, turn to **239**.

57

There's no disguising the fact that this guy is genuinely scared of these people. It takes a combination of wheedling, growling, and browbeating, but eventually you learn that the Australian seems to possess some unusual reserves of strength, mobility, and savagery, and he is working with at least one other person, an older man. They're holed up in a disused hotel in a slummy part of the city.

As something of a peace gesture, he offers you a pressurized can of [Illegal Pepper Spray], which you may take if you wish, and the ACHIEVEMENT: *Gumshoe*.

Heading back to the car, She-Hulk says, "We can't really stealth up in a car. So we either park down the street and approach on foot, or we just high-tail it up to the door and pile out. Which would you pick?"

To approach on foot, turn to **217**.
To zoom up in the car, turn to **130**.

58

Jen nods, and even though she doesn't move a muscle, she suddenly feels incredibly menacing, like a tornado a mile wide is barreling straight toward you and it's too late to even think of running. "Be very, very careful what you ask for." Her voice sounds cold and hollow. "You might receive it."

Teena's eyes go wide.

Make an intimidation test. Roll one die, and add your **POWER** to it.

Get 7 or more: Teena goes pale. "I'm sorry. I really am. Just don't hurt me. I'll leave." She immediately starts pulling off the jewelry and dumping it at her feet. A moment later, she's off, moving surprisingly quickly. As soon as she's gone, Jen grins, and that terrifying sense of power just clicks off. "That was quite satisfying," she says. Take **+1 POWER**.

On a 6 or less: Teena growls, backs up two feet, and begins a lumbering charge, massive ring-laden fists ready to fly. Jen steps forward, one arm out, and catches Teena by the top of the head. The big woman grunts, but she can't even get close enough to punch. She pushes harder, and Jen twists out of the way, using the woman's own weight to send her flying out the door. After twenty feet, Teena slows for a moment, and then just keeps going, off into the grounds. Jen shrugs.

"Now, according to the floorplan, the kitchens lead on to the parlor and the dining room," Jen says. "Preferences?"

"How about the parlor?" Turn to **292**.

"Let's try the dining room." Turn to **3**.

59

You've only been in the dreary visiting room for a couple of minutes when Ruby is shown in. She's medium height, with an athletic build and a shock of long, red hair. You'd put her in her early thirties, maybe, and pretty in a somewhat stern-looking way. She accepts the guard's direction to your table gracefully, and sits down. "Thanks for coming, Ms Walters. I appreciate it."

"Just Jen," She-Hulk says breezily. "We're all old enemies here. Speaking of, would you mind indulging me for a moment? I prefer to be sure."

A slow, surprisingly wicked grin spreads over her face. She looks straight at you, and then her entire head fades out like the Cheshire Cat, leaving behind a shiny red ball the size of a melon on top of a golden collar. "And you must call me Ruby," the red orb says. You have no idea where her voice is coming from. For a moment, the smooth surface sprouts dozens of sharp red spikes about a foot long, and then they vanish again. "I've been practicing." A long tentacle lashes out of the orb toward you and before you can flinch, it gently pushes your jaw back up, closing your mouth. "Rude to gawp, my dear," she tells you. The tentacle retracts, and to your great relief, her previous head fades back into existence, still smirking at you.

Jen shudders, just a little. If your {REASONABLE DOUBT} is 6 or less, turn to immediately to **216**.

Otherwise, she sets her shoulders. "Too much about this case doesn't make sense, Ruby. If you really were behind it, it would be smarter. Much smarter. So yes, I'll represent you. If you have any idea of what's going on behind the scenes though, now is the time to tell me. I am going to find out, and if I don't like it, I am going to stop it."

Ruby spreads her hands in a puzzled gesture. "Thank you. I have absolutely no idea why anyone would want me in county jail of all places, I promise you."

"I've been doing a bit of digging around," Jen says.

"Yes, I've heard. I like your work ethic." If your {WAVES} is 3 or more, take **+1** {SIMPATICO}.

If you want to pick over all of the details now, turn to **208**.

If you'd rather summarize, turn to **246**.

60

You head into the depths of the library. It's claustrophobic and a little unsettling, and as you walk past shelf after shelf, you note that it is *still* all paranormal romance, just not all in English. It's an impressive collection. Just how many languages would a computer-headed super-genius be able to read anyway?

Make a spot hidden things test. Roll one die, and add your **CONCENTRATION** to it.

Total of 8 or more: Between two books whose spines are in an alphabet you don't know, you see a **[Slim File]**. You may take it if you wish.

Eventually, you come to the end of the aisle. "This door leads to the cloakrooms," Jen says. "But we can try the gala room if you prefer."

For the cloakrooms, turn to **291**.

For the gala room, turn to **27**.

61

You walk into the woods. Little by little, the track gets narrower and more overgrown as you progress. You're starting to think you made a mistake when the path opens up into a wide, carefully tended clearing. Standing around this space are a dozen gleaming stone owl statues. The shortest is over five feet high, and the tallest over seven.

They don't seem to be in any particular pattern, but the tall one is closest to the center of the clearing. You stare at them. One or two are positioned to stare back.

She-Hulk frowns. "What exactly is going on here?"

Take +1 {REASONABLE DOUBT}.

The central statue appears to be holding something. You approach, and see that the mystery object is another owl statue, palm-sized this time. There's something... squirmy about it.

Make a resolve test. Roll one die, and add your **POWER** to it.

7 or more: You make take the [Squirmy Owlet] with you if you like.

6 or less: Your thoughts re repelled by the statuette. Take -1 CONCENTRATION.

Now, there's no way onwards, so you'll have to backtrack.

For the concrete path, turn to **42**.

To take the pleasant walkway, turn to **164**.

62

At a first glance, the pool area looks like an archetypical indoor swimming pool – large, airy room, decent-sized swimming pool of white stone with metal ladders in and out, slatted wooden benches along the walls, even a few big plants in planters. There's a flabby guy standing on the water in the middle of the pool. That gives you pause, until you realize that the water is only an inch deep, and the rest is just careful painting.

The man is wearing an unflatteringly tight brown one-piece costume with a rainbow-colored "W" symbol on his chest, and darker boots and gauntlets. The mask that covers most of his head has a yellow face with thick whiskers, a pair of tusks descending past his chin, and a black button nose. In his meaty hands he cradles a chunky hammer decorated with a stylized shrieking face and a glowing handle.

How well-warned are your enemies at this point? If your {WATCHED} is between 1 and 3, set your {PENALTY} to 1. If it is 4 to 6, set {PENALTY} to 2. If it's 7 or more, set {PENALTY} to 3.

"Walrus!" She-Hulk says. "I shouldn't be disappointed, given how things have been going, but here we are."

"Your rampage stops here, She-Hulk," Walrus says. He sounds like a cabbie from the Bronx.

"Oh, I wouldn't call it a *rampage*." Her voice drops from pleasant to menacing. "Not yet."

"Yeah, well, you're about to be the… 5th notch on my hammer today." He starts splashing forward, swinging the hammer in wide circles.

Jen looks at you. "Mr Carpenter is not supposed to be particularly dangerous. His boast is typically that he's got the proportional strength and resilience of a real walrus. Since he's a lot smaller than a real walrus, it's a sad claim, the poor man. How would you deal with him?"

"Disarm him." Turn to **240**.

"Jump him." Turn to **293**.

63

The scroll door leads into a square, futuristic room that leans heavily on hard white plastic, brightly colorful LED light strips, and brushed steel. The walls display circuit-like patterns, and there are no obvious exits. A metal desk in the middle of the room contains an embedded display showing a complex design, a network of pipes and valves.

You walk over to it, and hear a tiny click. Make a reflex test. Roll one die and add your **CONCENTRATION** and **POWER**. A guillotine blade plummets down out of the ceiling toward you! Quick, what's your total?

15 or more, or if you have {**MICROSWITCHED**} of 1: She-Hulk pulls you back out of danger.

14 or less: She manages to get a hand in place to stop the blade from severing your head, but it hurts. Take **-1 POWER** and **-1 CHARM**.

A pair of doors light up on the walls, bearing geometric sigils. How would you like to progress?

For the triangle door, turn to **46**.

For the square door, turn to **247**.

64

If the guest suite was unusual, the library is downright weird. There are no windows at all, and the room must be as tall as the entire building. Careful use – and denial – of light give the impression that it vanishes on upwards into darkness. The bookcases are all dark wrought iron, lacy but solid. To the front of the room, the cases are spread out to give a more open feel, and there are some reading desks there, topped in green leather, with small lamps on them. Further in, the shelving is packed together tightly, dim and forbidding.

It really does look like a temple to forbidden knowledge. You glance at a nearby shelf, and the first book you see is titled *Oh My Beast*. A closer examination suggests everything around it is, well, in the paranormal romance genre. Ruby Thursday has a soft side? Huh.

To press on into the gloomy depths of the library, turn to **60**.

To head to the gala room instead, turn to **27**.

65

You park up and do a circuit of the compound on foot. It's larger than you expected, a lot quieter too. You'd expect a site holding hundreds of workers to have a buzz to it, but there's nothing.

While you don't find any back entrance on your circuit, you do discover a reasonably big telecommunications cabinet that obviously provides hard-lines to the complex, and possibly some of its power as well. It won't be the only source of either, but taking it out of service might help make things easier for you inside.

If you have {LEISURELY RESPONSE} of 1, you notice a police cruiser not too far from you, watching your activities quietly, so sabotage is impossible. Turn back to **18** and choose something else.

Otherwise, She-Hulk can try breaking the cabinet. Take **+1 POWER** and then make a useful force test. Roll one die and add your **POWER**. If the total is 8 or more, she breaks some important connections, so take **+1 {NOBBLED}**.

Now, if you have {DELIVERY PATTERNS} of 1, you can try intercepting groceries by turning to **273**.

If you have {FOOD TRUCK} of 1 and want to try talking your way onto a sandwich van, turn to **97**.

Or, to scale the wall, turn to **119**.

66

The spare room is a cluttered warren of boxes and high-end suitcases. It would be quite refreshingly normal, in fact, if it wasn't for the small bomb in the middle of the floor. As you look at it, it chirps, and a light comes on in the electronic mess surrounding the brick of Semtex. Well, it says "Semtex" on the label, anyway.

She-Hulk mutters something, and grabs it.

Make a trap! test. Roll one die and add your **CONCENTRATION**.

7 or more: She pulls a couple of metal plugs out of the explosive, shaking her head.

6 or more: She flings the device straight through the window. An instant later, there's a huge explosion, and dust obscures everything. As your hearing returns, you think you hear rubble settling. Take **+2 {WAVES}** and the ACHIEVEMENT: *Bringing Down the House.*

"Amateurs." Jen sounds thoroughly disgusted.

After all that, the room is useless. It's all decorations, cleaning supplies, and other house-related things.

To search the master bedroom, turn to **85**.

To look at the guest bedroom, turn to **235**.

To check the bathroom, turn to **271**.

67

This is the odd one out! Well done! Why 67 is the odd one out depends on where you came from – via the kitchens, it's not a square or a cube; via the snack bar, it's a prime, and via the guest suite, it's not a multiple of 17. Alternatively, if you got here by solving the puzzle, take **+1 {PUZZLER}** and the ACHIEVEMENT: *The Odd One.*

"That's not me," Jen says. "I'm not odd."

You arch an eyebrow, but say nothing.

However you got here, you are now in Ruby's secure home office suite, surrounded by computer equipment – and you are not alone. Across the room, there is a tall, square-jawed fellow with broad shoulders and a thin, curly mustache of the sort favored by classic villains. He's wearing a flowing green coat covered with stars, which he's paired, distressingly, with magenta trousers. His top hat matches the trews, and boasts a distracting swirly disk that spins of its own accord. He's talking to a slender, red-haired little man in bright clothes and big pink glasses.

"Hello, Maynard," Jen says. "How are the eyes?" You notice that she looks away from him as he turns, so you do the same. That disk is *very* swirly.

"Please, my dear Glamazonia, you know I prefer Ringmaster." You're not looking, but you can hear the smirk on his face. "You're looking a little staid today, if I may. But thank you, my eyes are better than ever. It's amazing what a couple of drops of healing factor serum can do."

Without looking, She-Hulk snatches up a solid-looking desktop computer case and tosses it at Ringmaster.

Make a tough throwing test. Roll one die and add your **POWER**.

On an 11 or more: The computer catches him in the stomach heavily, and he collapses. She-Hulk leaps behind him, flings his hat across the room, pulls his coat over his face, and forces him to the ground. Turn to **294**.

10 or less: Ringmaster steps out of the way, tutting smugly. Turn to **189**.

Once you're both in the antechamber, you press the button. The lab door swooshes closed, there's a beep, red light floods the room briefly, and the corridor door opens. You head on through. It seems like a lot of fuss for a corridor, honestly. Although, now you're in here, you notice that the walls and ceiling are slightly curved, and there are small circular windows onto dark rooms spaced regularly along it. The overall effect leaves you feeling a bit floaty. The lights are back in the ceiling, at least.

Something in one of the windows catches your eye, and you look more closely.

Oh. Oh.

It's not a dark room out there after all. It's the blackness of space. The glittering stars scattered across the empty void are a complete giveaway. What the…?

"Watch out," Jen says. She sounds unusually tense.

A horrible ball of thin, flailing tentacles is rolling down the corridor toward you at high speed. It's at least five feet in diameter, and if there's a solid core – anything at all apart from those tendrils – it's well hidden. Another one is close behind it. As they get close, they leap, engulfing She-Hulk in a mass of writhing nastiness.

This is a tricky fight.

Round one: roll two dice, add your power, and subtract your {SPACE ALERT} if any. If the total is 12 or more, you win the first round.

Round two: roll two dice, add your power, and subtract

your {SPACE ALERT} if any. If the total is 12 or more, you win the second round.

She-Hulk manages to rip her attackers to shreds in the end, but if you lost at least one round, and you are *not* wearing the [Odd Helmets], then take -1 CHARM, -2 CONCENTRATION, and +1 {SHAKEN}.

While she's recovering from the attack, you have a moment.

To look more carefully out of a window, turn to **93**.

To examine the dead creatures, turn to **234**.

69

Jen doesn't turn around when you shout out, but she does call back, "Right." She dances back a couple of steps, then launches herself off the floor, straight at the eye, one fist outstretched.

The abomination flinches back, but a moment later, the eye explodes, showering the entire room in truly disgusting goo, you included. The thing starts flailing around, and eerie purple energies crackle over its surface.

Make a resilience test. Roll one die and add your POWER and CONCENTRATION.

If you have {ILLUMINATED} of 1, or the total is 13 or more, take -1 CHARM.

If the total is 12 or less, take -2 CHARM, -2 CONCENTRATION, and -2 POWER.

In less than thirty seconds, the abomination has dissolved into a huge, revolting pool of sticky ooze. She-

Hulk is standing in the middle of the pool, looking annoyed, slimy, and thoroughly grossed out. Add the ACHIEVEMENT: *Smashing*.

Now, to examine the remains and the archway, turn to **102**.

To examine the computer equipment, turn to **116**.

70

"Friendly," you mutter. Jen nods, and slows her walk, relaxing her stance. She walks up to the desk and sits in one of the chairs facing it. You take the other.

"Thanks for seeing us, Judge Hirst," Jen says gently. "I don't believe that you involved yourself in my client's case voluntarily. You know who I am. Whatever leverage they have on you, I can get you out of this. But I can't do it unless you trust me." Take **+1 CHARM**.

The judge visibly wavers. "I would be happy to revise Ms Rubinstein's case after the weekend." She sounds irresolute.

"Too late. These people have murdered at least one hundred and twenty people in Silicon Valley over the last three months, and their plan comes to a head this week."

The judge gasps and goes an unhealthy shade of grey. "One hundred and... Dear lord... My sister. They have my sister. Marion. They said... Get her back, I beg you."

"Who?"

"I don't know. They took her outside a bar. She was going to meet an ex. He might know something. I also asked some quiet questions, and there's a CI who's often round that area. He's another possibility. I didn't dare risk it, but…"

Jen spends some time comforting the judge, and assuring her that everything will be fine.

To find Marion's ex, turn to **5**.

To find the informant, turn to **212**.

71

The compound opens up around the side of the main building. There are a number of smaller, office-like structures, all set in grounds styled to suggest a Japanese park without ever quite committing. It's pretty though, apart from the drones screeching across the sky. For the moment, at least, they're not attacking. A path that leads from the ornamental lake runs to the main building here, and a big, secure-looking door, complete with entry keypad.

This is a puzzle! What is 6+7*17-3*(30/9)+2?

The answer is "117": turn to **159**.

"193": turn to **134**.

"728.6": turn to **19**.

72

Kangaroo flies across the road and into the building opposite, crashing a huge hole in the wall of what must surely be a condemned apartment block. You really hope it's condemned. You hear a muffled "Crikey!" She-Hulk jumps after him, doing some more structural damage. A moment later she reappears, flying through the air with Kangaroo held out in front of her, upside down. They land in the middle of the street in a perfect, if savage, piledriver.

As they thump down, the entire front of the apartment block gives up and collapses. Many of the rooms are indeed abandoned, but there is a group very startled, seedy-looking middle-aged men suddenly missing a front wall. Take +2 {WAVES}.

Kangaroo groans and collapses. She-Hulk rips his metal tail off, pulls out several feet of stout wiring from inside it, and trusses him up like a roasting pig. You can let She-Hulk catch her breath, or start in on interrogating Kangaroo.

For a breather, turn to **124**.

To talk to the Australian, turn to **168**.

73

The man puts his laser down. "Now you let me go?" he asks hopefully.

She-Hulk laughs. "Now I don't rip your arms and legs off. Go on, sit down."

Once the man is blindfolded, the last bits of defiance go out of him. He identifies himself as Cool Million, and says he was hired through a mercenary broker to keep this site locked down. It's perfectly obvious that he has hypnotic powers, but he insists on telling you all about them in excruciating detail anyway. Seriously. Has anyone ever cared that he got started practicing on chickens?

Take +1 {REASONABLE DOUBT} and the ACHIEVEMENT: *Not So Cool Now, Huh?*

The Omni and Grey people start coming round, perfectly normal again but really angry, and it's tense for a few minutes until She-Hulk persuades them that the authorities are the right people to take it from here.

The staff happily give you Anthony Bright's files – the ones that aren't commercially sensitive anyway. One of the files contains a weird [Fungal Token] that you can take if you like.

If any of your POWER, CHARM, or CONCENTRATION are below 2, set them to 2 now. If you still have a mug of [Coffee] with you, you may safely drink it for a further +1 CONCENTRATION. Finally, take +1 CHARM and +1 CONCENTRATION for saving the devs, and set {FILES} to 1.

> If you want to search Bright's home and haven't done so, turn to **185**.
>
> If you want to start putting the pieces together, turn to **252**.

74

You go over to the staff café and enter. No one leaps out to tell you that you shouldn't. It's a large, vaguely Nordic-looking space – lots of pine, white walls and modern-looking furniture, all clean lines and brisk efficiency. Pleasant smells of fresh coffee and hot baked goods waft from the counter, which is staffed by a smiling barista. The place is quietly busy, with a low buzz of conversation. Everyone looks cheerful, and while there's obviously no uniform, you see a lot of monochrome t-shirts, jeans, and plaid. They all completely ignore you, in an oblivious sort of way, rather than a mean-girls-in-college way. You could easily be in Portland.

Most people are in small groups, but there are a couple of loners. Jen looks at you expectantly.

"Let's talk to someone." Turn to **35**.

"How about a coffee?" Turn to **90**.

75

The main entrance is definitely understated. No red carpet, no big signs, no greeters, just a pair of frosted glass doors with *VIP* stenciled on them – and several large, poorly-besuited thugs holding futuristic automatic weapons loitering around. Jen frowns. "That's a very strange amount of firepower for a Con. Even in a distant corridor like this in one of *these* books. I blame the Brits."

Wait, what? "What did they do?"

"It's more what they *didn't* do."

You shrug. There's a pass-scanner next to the door, along with what looks like a palm-reader. On the ceiling, you notice the domes of several security cameras, placed to ensure good line of sight of anyone approaching.

"We've got a couple of possible approaches here," Jen says. "I can try leaning on Ruby's company as a ticket in, or I can try bullying the guards – there's no way the Expo is on the DOJ assault weapons list."

"Let's try using Thurstech." Turn to **286**.

"Let's try the legal approach." Turn to **112**.

"Let's try the staff entrance." Turn to **17**.

76

Whichever goblet you selected in the last entry, She-Hulk picks it up, raises it to you in a sardonic toast, and drinks. "Tastes like water." She has another swig. "If there's anything bad in there, it's about as subtle as Iocane."

ACHIEVEMENT: *Sip of Faith.*

A spotlight flicks on, shining down onto the space in front of the plinth. Symbols appear in the light – an ellipsis, a plus sign, and another ellipsis. Then the light winks out.

"Enigmatic," you say.

"Maybe it'll be relevant later," she says. "I wouldn't get your hopes up though, not in a book like this."

"What?"

"Oh, nothing."

Up ahead, vine-covered wall panels slide away to reveal a pair of doors onwards. They have plaques this time. One says *Temple*, the other *Pool*.

For the temple, turn to **166**.

For the pool, turn to **62**.

77

She-Hulk clutches at her head, and sinks to her knees. "Leave. My. Ugh. Mind. Alone." Her words are strained and slow.

"I think not," Ringmaster gloats.

Do you have a [Chunk of Robot]? It was constructed of quite exotic material. You try holding it in front of Jen's face to block the Ringmaster's hypnotic powers. She gasps in relief, and takes it, holding it like a shield. Turn to **231**.

Otherwise, make a last-ditch mental resistance test. Roll one die and add your CONCENTRATION.

On a 9 or more: turn to **231**.

8 or less: Alas, She-Hulk sags, then stands up smoothly. Her expression is completely blank. As you stare at her in horror, you feel your own consciousness fading. Darkness falls. ACHIEVEMENT: *Puppet Masters*.

The end.

78

"I'll try, but like I said, it's tough," Jen says. "Stay back." She lowers her head, balls her fists, and charges toward Bi-Beast. At the last moment, she jumps to smash into it at chest height, battering at its head. It reaches up and flings her off. She-Hulk rolls as she lands, comes back up, and moves back on the attack.

This is a very hard fight.

Round one: roll two dice, add your **POWER**, and subtract your {PENALTY}. If the total is 14 or more, you win the first round.

Round two: roll two dice, add your **POWER**, and subtract your {PENALTY}. If the total is 14 or more, you win the second round.

Round three: roll two dice, add your **POWER**, and subtract your {PENALTY}. If the total is 14 or more, you win the third round.

If you won at least one round, turn to **180**.

If you lost all three rounds, turn to **36**.

79

She-Hulk rolls out of the way of the robot's next attack, then leaps back several feet to regroup. She turns to the side, wrenching one of the wooden benches out of the ground. A chunk of concrete sticks to each end, and beneath the wood, you can see some sturdy metalwork. As the robot readies its sword, she steps forward, swinging the bench like it was a baseball bat.

This is a boss fight.

Round one: roll two dice and add your **POWER** and, if you have any, your {TROUBLESOME}. If the total is 13 or more, you win the first round.

Round two: roll two dice and add your **POWER** and, if you have any, your {TROUBLESOME} and your {NOBBLED}. If the total is 14 or more, you win the second round.

Round three: roll two dice and add your **POWER** and, if you have any, your {TROUBLESOME} and your {NOBBLED}. If the total is 15 or more, you win the third round.

Subtract 1 from the number of rounds you won, and adjust your **POWER** by that much: that could range from **+2** if you won all three, to **-1** if you lost all three.

The bench shatters, and She-Hulk's expression is grim, but the robot is looking a little dented. You want to help, but which potential weak-spot are you going to suggest?

"Go for the neck!" Turn to **110**.

"Go for the power core!" Turn to **162**.

80

"How very sweet of you," Ruby says. "I've actually enjoyed my time here greatly. No emails, no calls, no Twitter, just R&R. Have you read Martha Wells? Something about her work really speaks to me. Maybe it's the name 'Murderbot.' If you're rich, jail can be extremely comfortable. And I am. Very. Besides, all the career criminals are utterly terrified I'm going to obliterate them if they put a toenail wrong, and that has its own charm."

Jen arches an eyebrow. "I can imagine."

You could ask why she doesn't break out by turning to **241**.

Alternatively, let She-Hulk ask about the bail situation; turn to **30**.

81

She-Hulk staggers for a moment, and shakes her head vigorously, like she's trying to knock something loose. "No," she grates out. "I've been whammied by better than you, buddy. Look, be clever here. That little cat toy isn't even going to sting, it's just going to make me angry. You wouldn't like that."

Make a persuasion roll. Roll one die and add your **CHARM**.

Get to 6 or more: turn to **73**.

5 or less: turn to **196**.

82

You solved the lectern! A is worth 24, B is 31, and C is 17, and 2A + 2C = 82. Well done! Take **+1 {PUZZLER}**. Impressive.

You say "Eighty two," and a loud chime sounds. Panels on either side of the auditorium slide up to reveal doors. One of them is decorated with a circle, the other with a square. Which do you prefer?

For the square door, turn to **247**.

For the circle door, turn to **215**.

"Jen Walters," she says, smiling pleasantly. "Thanks for talking with us, Mr Winton. It's good to meet you. I was hoping you might be able to help me regarding Anthony Bright."

Make a charm test. Roll one die, and add your **CHARM** to it. If your total is 7 or more, take **+1 CHARM**.

"Poor Tony," Winton says sadly. "A tragic and senseless loss. He was a brilliant software engineer, and a dear personal friend. Death is always cruel, don't you think? Especially so when it claims the young. So much to live for, so vibrant, and then suddenly all that promise is cut short. The world can be a senseless place. That's why we exist, you know. We want to help things make sense. This campus is a haven, a place designed to make sense. It's so important to make sense, don't you think? But of course you do, how could it be otherwise. I'm so glad we got the chance to have this little chat. I do understand how busy you are however, so I'll let you get on with it."

"Okay." Jen sounds thoughtful. "Thanks."

She turns around, and you follow her out. Off to one side, you note a bulky surveillance cam watching you. Take **+1 {COOL}**.

As soon as you get outside, she stops. "That was curious." Take **+1 {REASONABLE DOUBT}**.

Paths lead off into the woodland behind the visitor's lodge, and there's no one immediately visible to tell you not to wander off. There's also the café, though.

To explore the grounds, turn to **223**.

To try the café if you haven't already, turn to **74**.

84

Congratulations on finding your way here!

ACHIEVEMENT: *Secret Six.*

The arena wall has been badly broken in several places, and looking at the hole the Thing made getting in, you spot several strands of cabling. You go through to the other side of the wall, and see that there are regularly-spaced speaker stacks facing the arena wall, connected with thick audio cable. There's a control panel up against the wall next to the tunnel entrance you came through, and although there's a lot about it you don't understand, there is a clear volume slider. You crank it all the way up, and Chtylok immediately warbles a pained "Kraaaw!"

Take +1 {OUCH!} then turn to **218**.

85

The master bedroom is large but reassuringly comfortable. The bed is huge and messy, the various tables and chests of drawers are littered with bits and pieces ranging from crumpled t-shirts to candy bars and cans of deodorant, and there's a chunky armchair looking out the window onto the back yard. A well-worn copy of Al Ewing's *You Are Deadpool* sits on its arm.

Five potted petunias sit on the windowsill near the

armchair. It's curious – nothing else you've seen so far has suggested that Bright has any interest in flowers.

You divide up the clutter between you, and start looking for anything that might provide some information. After a couple of minutes, an old-fashioned wall telephone starts ringing loudly. She-Hulk looks at it, then shrugs and answers. "Bright residence, Ms Walters speaking. No, I'm a lawyer. Something like that, yes. No, I haven't heard anything untoward. Yes, of course. Thank you."

Make a persuasion test. Roll one die and add your **CHARM**. If the total is 7 or less, take **+1 {LEISURELY RESPONSE}**.

She hangs up. "Just a security company. They assumed I was assessing the estate. I think they bought it. They did if the roll went well, anyway."

You get back to searching. It takes half an hour, but finally you're sure there's nothing helpful in here. Take **+1 {DELAYED}**.

To move on to the bathroom, turn to **271**.

To check the guest bedroom, turn to **235**.

To try the spare room, turn to **66**.

86

She-Hulk blinks, and shakes her head groggily. She lashes out at Bessie, but the vampire just takes a step back and laughs her awful, mooing laugh. You note with curiosity that she still has her original teeth as well as her curved, gleaming fangs, but her tongue is much longer and thinner than it should be. You're going to have to have words with your subconscious when you wake up.

Then Bessie is lashing out with a savagely fast razor hoof to the face. Jen just manages to jerk her head out of the way in time and the blow doesn't quite land. They exchange a flurry of blows, attacks and blocks and counterpunches, but She-Hulk is forced back several steps.

This is a fight!

Round one: roll two dice and add your **POWER**. If the total is 9 or more, you win the first round.

Round two: roll two dice and add your **POWER**. If you won the first round, add 1. If the total is 8 or more, you win the second round.

If you won that second round, turn to **201**.

If you lost the second round, turn to **55**.

87

"I guess," Jen says. "I'll do what I can. Keep away from that monster." She takes a couple of steps back, then sprints forward and jumps, hurtling through to air to catch hold of one of the pillars part-way down the temple. Bi-Beast pauses then strides toward her, but before it can get close, Jen jumps again, hurtling across to the other side of the temple, and then immediately leaps once more, landing behind the android. As it twists, she smashes into it.

This is a hard fight.

Round one: roll two dice, add your **POWER**, and subtract your {PENALTY}. If you have a [Stained Machete], add **+2**. If the total is 12 or more, you win the first round.

Round two: roll two dice, add your **POWER**, and subtract your {PENALTY}. If you have a [Stained Machete]. If the total is 12 or more, you win the second round.

If you won both rounds, turn to **49**.

If you lost any rounds, turn to **180**.

88

Away from the main trade halls, the Expo is a lot saner. It's a bewildering maze, but there's room to breathe and think. You've been wandering around for twenty minutes when Jen points out an elegant lady ahead in a black dress, carrying a briefcase. "That's Isabella Cruz. She's a ferocious privacy activist: doctorates from two different law schools, bylines in several major newspapers, the works. Come on." She speeds up to catch her.

"Ms Cruz," she says breezily as she gets close. "Jennifer Walters, atto–"

The woman turns, and smiles. "You need no introduction, She-Hulk. It is a delight."

"Jen, please, and the honor is mine. I'm a huge fan." The

feeling proves mutual, and the pair spend several minutes chatting. Then Jen's face darkens. "Bella, are you headed to the VIP area?"

"Yes," the other says. "Why?"

"Yeah… Listen: it's a trap. A lethal one. A major criminal is running this year's Expo, and there's a monster so powerful in there that it worried Mr Fantastic. You *can't* go in. If I wasn't scared of triggering a catastrophic response, I'd be trying to get the whole Center evacuated."

Isabella's eyes narrow. "How can I help?"

"Stay safe first, try to keep others away from VIP second – and tell me where the damn entry to the VIP area actually is."

"Done." She pulls a site map from her briefcase, a detailed one. "The entrance is here, in 9H. I will try to find reliable people to cover all three approaches, and yes, I will be cautious."

"Thank you," Jen says. "I look forward to talking with you more under less… explosive circumstances."

There are two doors into the map's featureless VIP area, one small and out of the way that is almost certainly for staff. Which do you prefer?

For the main entrance, turn to **75**.

For the staff entrance, turn to **17**.

89

You drop Exie off at a quaint house in the Bay Area that she describes as "completely safe." She's quite nice really, for a powerful tech CEO with deep ties to the defense sector, paranoid ideation, CPTSD, and a shiny new phobia of robots. Fortunately she can afford to get a lot of very expensive help with all that.

The pair of you go back to San José, and the next morning, you head downtown to the county jail, where Ruby is still being held. It's a large, blocky white building with multiple towers, right in the heart of the civic center, near the airport and several major highways. It takes a minute or two for Jen to handshake her way through the startled guards and attendants and into the building, but they're well-used to lawyers and paralegals here, if not to super heroes. It's dazzling to watch her in action, simultaneously charming, businesslike, pleasant, and ever so slightly terrifying. She's one heck of a lawyer.

In short order, Ruby Thursday is on her way to the visitors' room, and you have a moment spare.

To just go in and wait, turn to **59**.

If you'd like to ask the staff about Ruby, turn to **123**.

Or, to freshen up, turn to **38**.

90

You head over to the counter. The barista is a professionally smiley young person with colorful hair and an unusually blissful expression. "Hey," they say.

"The coffee smells good," Jen says.

"It's wonderful. Two coffees. Something to eat?"

They turn, and deftly slip a couple of espresso holders

into the machine, which starts gurgling. A big surveillance cam swivels to watch you. Take **+1 {COOL}**.

"Just the coffee, thanks. Can we get them to go?"

"Go?"

"Yeah, you know, to take outside."

"Oh!" They brighten. "You can take them wherever you like."

"Great." She sounds careful now. "How much do I owe you?"

"We are one," the barista says brightly, and puts two mugs of coffee in front of you.

"Of course," Jen says. "We are one."

The barista beams at her. Take **+1 {REASONABLE DOUBT}**.

You pick up your coffees and walk away. You may choose to keep your **[Coffee]** –Jen puts hers down on a table and backs away. "How would you proceed?" she asks.

To head out the back and explore, turn to **223**.

To talk to an employee, turn to **23**.

If you haven't already, to visit the lodge, turn to **152**.

91

She-Hulk pushes Walrus away, ruining his balance. She follows up with a punch, but he fends it off with the hammer, then lashes a blow at her neck. She steps back, and he flings himself at her, his weapon smashing into her knee. Take **-1 POWER**. She curses and staggers back, and to your surprise, Walrus turns and runs. He's fast, too. Before Jen is mobile again, he's gone through the door you came in from.

Jen limps up to you painfully, shaking her head. "Annoying as that was, he's not the priority. Our spider will be at the center of this web. We should press on."

The far end of the room opens up into a changing area with a shower unit, beyond which you see a couple of doors. One is stenciled with a coffee cup, the other with a washbasin.

"What do you think?" She-Hulk asks.

"I could use a coffee." Turn to **299**.

"How about the washroom?" Turn to **26**.

92

Tekeli Industries occupies an entire block in Mountain View. There are tall gray stone walls with regular security cameras, punctuated by a single small gatehouse. Behind the barred gate, you can see a traffic island with an ornamental fountain where the road divides into two and heads into some trees. A tall, undistinguished office building lurks behind them.

The guard in the gatehouse looks tired and put-upon, but after delivering a double-take at Jen that seems to wake him right up, he manages to greet you pleasantly enough. "Delivery for Neil Gould," Jen tells him.

The guard glances at his clipboard. "It's not scheduled."

"It's the Thurstech usual," she says, following Ruby's instructions. Make a persuasion test. Roll one die and add your **CHARM**.

Get a 7 or more: turn to **229**.

6 or less: turn to **141**.

93

You're not an astronomer, but you have at least at vague idea of what the night sky looks like, and what you see through the window isn't … right. Earth's sky is quite crowded, even if you're not actually looking at the Milky Way. The space outside this corridor is much emptier. There are lots of stars, sure, but nothing like enough. Somehow, you are a very, *very* long way from home.

Take +1 {**SHAKEN**} and the ACHIEVEMENT: *Lost In Space.*

Jen sighs. "At least there's no Jonathan Harris."

If you still want to examine the attackers, turn to **234**.

If you'd rather continue on up the corridor, turn to **163**.

94

The fountain sits in a circle of path, benches surrounding it. It's a simple thing, a basin with a tall spout that is currently not pumping any water. A disheveled man in a well-worn suit is lying on one of the benches, blinking at the pair of you as he slowly wakes up.

Jen goes over to him. "Hey there. You here often?"

He stares at her for a long moment, then blinks slowly, stares again, and finally shakes his head slowly. You know the feeling. "That a problem, lady?" he asks, but he just sounds beaten rather than aggressive.

"Jen. And no, not at all. Were you here three nights ago?"

He nods wearily. "Monday. Yeah, *Jen*, I was here. Work the night shift, see. Warehouse is just down the hill. My buddies will be here soon, but they're on lates tonight."

"Did you see a couple come by here, tech types, late? She probably had red hair, an expensive suit. He was young and scruffy."

The man frowns.

"Don't botch this," Jen murmurs. "I'm plenty charming."

"Pardon?" you ask.

"Not you," she smiles.

Make a persuasion test. Roll one die, and add your **CHARM** to it. On a 5 or more: He shakes his head. "No. I was here by six. Some guys, sure. Definitely no women. You're rare here after dark." Take **+1 {REASONABLE DOUBT}** and **+1 CHARM**.

4 or less: He shrugs. "Didn't notice anyone either way. Sorry."

She nods. "You've been very helpful …?"

"Todd," the man says. "You're welcome, I guess."

"Have a beer on me?" she asks.

"Sure, thanks," Todd says.

She fishes in her bag, and pulls out a couple of notes, which she hands over.

Todd looks at them slowly, then smiles broadly. "That's one *heck* of a beer, Jen."

"You're welcome," she says. "Least I can do." Then she turns to you. "So, what next?"

"The murder site." Turn to **282**.

"The trees." Turn to **237**.

"The lampposts." Turn to **269**.

95

There's no disguising the fact that the guy is genuinely scared of these people. It takes a combination of wheedling, growling, and browbeating, but eventually you learn that the Australian is holed up in a disused hotel in a slummy part of the city.

Take **+1 {FLAT-FOOTED}**.

Heading back to the car, She-Hulk says, "We can't really stealth up in a car. So we either park down the street and approach on foot, or we high-tail it up to the door and pile out. Which would you pick?"

To approach on foot, turn to **217**.

To zoom up in the car, turn to **130**.

96

Yes, all four words are ways of expressing different meanings of the word "set". Well done! Take **+1 CONCENTRATION**, **+1 {PUZZLER}**, and **+1 {REASONABLE DOUBT}**.

Bright had been very scared, and with good reason. In the last three months he'd tracked more than a hundred untimely deaths clustered around six companies – including both Thurstech, and Omni and Grey.

These events started almost immediately after the suicide of a famous tech visionary, Sturm Vanguard. It's clear that Vanguard had been looking to invest in all six of the companies before his death. All of their CEOs, including Ruby, had meetings at his sprawling personal compound. Since his death, the compound has gone into an enigmatic lockdown.

Bright was obviously thinking about getting inside. His notes include the compound's daily grocery delivery and its food truck schedule. Set **{DELIVERY PATTERNS}** and **{FOOD TRUCK}** to 1 each. He also referred to a third source that catalogued some of the compound's defenses, which apparently include drones, turrets, and other automated security.

To investigate the defenses, turn to **153**.

To dig deeper into the six companies, turn to **233**.

To research Vanguard further, turn to **238**.

97

Anthony Bright's notes include a local deli truck that is allowed into the complex twice a day. The van is usually on the downtown strip, near the town square, and that's where you find it.

Becca, the van's owner, is a sweet-natured young woman, and she's deeply troubled by the idea of smuggling people into Vanguard. When Jen expresses her concerns about the place and asks her how busy it is in there, her expression turns troubled. "They've always paid me a flat fee to turn up. I've only seen one person there over the last month, though. The new boss. She's come down for a BLT maybe five times in total?"

"I'm worried for her," Jen says. You at least know she's telling the truth.

Take **+1 CHARM** and make a persuasion test. Roll one die and add your **CHARM**. If the total is 7 or more, Becca not only drives you inside, but she gives you both delicious sandwiches to enjoy as well. Mmm, sandwiches. Turn immediately to **202**.

If not, she apologetically refuses. You'll have to try something else.

> If you have {DELIVERY PATTERNS} of 1, you can try intercepting groceries by turning to **273**.
>
> To scale the wall, turn to **119**.

98

Why yes, this is a secret entrance to the VIP area. "H" is the eighth letter, so *98*. Very nicely done! ACHIEVEMENT: *Secret Five*.

Now, you thread through a small warren of disused conference rooms and stretches of corridor to a simple wooden door. It's being held open by a gaming prop, a twelve-sided crystal the size of your fist. You may take it if you want. While the [Crystal Dodecahedron] is in your inventory, you get +1 to POWER, CHARM and CONCENTRATION, but you may also destroy it the one time to win any one test or one round of a fight.

You walk through the door into a small stretch of beige corridor. There are three frosted glass doors at the other end, one directly ahead and the other two set in the walls opposite each other. One is red, one is green, and one is blue.

"I've got a bad feeling about this," Jen says. "What's your favorite color?"

"Red." Turn to **194**.

"Green." Turn to **178**.

"Blue." Turn to **298**.

99

She-Hulk ducks and twists, and her hand flashes up to grab the hammer's handle. It stops dead in mid-swing, and Walrus's own momentum wrenches it out of his grip as he keeps moving. She immediately springs away from him, and smashes the handle over her knee, breaking it near the hammer head. The glow vanishes. Walrus wails, then sinks to his knees.

Thirty seconds later, Walrus is tied up securely with the ripped-off arms and legs of his own costume. Wow, his skin is really pale and unhealthy-looking under there. He doesn't even struggle, he just lies there in despair at the destruction of his hammer.

Take **+1 POWER** and the ACHIEVEMENT: *This is for the Oysters.*

Ignoring Walrus, you look around the room for ways onward. The far end of the room opens up into a changing area with a shower unit, beyond which you see a couple of doors. One is stenciled with a coffee cup, the other with a washbasin.

"What do you think?" She-Hulk asks.

"I could use a coffee." Turn to **299**.

"How about the washroom?" Turn to **26**.

100

"I tuned out the irrelevant details. That's a survival skill when you're dealing with Reed. But the basics are that there's someone or something ridiculously powerful in this conference center, and he can't get a lock on it. Exact position, exact nature, it's fuzzy. Being deliberately suppressed, he reckons. All he can tell is that it's Hulk-grade. I've stomped round the center twice, waving this silly little techno-wand sensor he gave me, and now I'm waiting for him to have a look at that data and get back to me."

Jen looks worried. "Think it's some surprise the guy I'm after has prepared?"

"No, it's a *total* coincidence," Ben deadpans. Take +1 {WHEELS WITHIN WHEELS}.

> To ask if Ben has any theories, turn to **132**.
>
> To ask what he knows about the Expo, turn to **142**.
>
> To suggest working together, turn to **198**.

101

The pack are thinning out when a loud buzzer sounds, and all the monitors in the room click on, each showing an intense pair of eyes. "Stand down, She-Hulk," a voice booms, echoing from all around you.

Make a luck roll. Roll one die. If you have a [Squirmy Owlet], add 3.

On a 4 or more: nothing happens.

3 or less: Whatever your {COOL} is, subtract that many points from your stats in any combination you choose. Note that you can't go below 0 this way, and hitting 0 does not have any immediate bad effects.

The remains of the pack are still attacking. Roll two

dice and add your **POWER** and, if you have any, your {TRANSFORMED}. If the total is 9 or less, take **-1 POWER** and **-1 CONCENTRATION** from the stress of dealing with these civilians. You can go below 0 this time.

As the last one falls, an office door opens at the back of the room, and a man comes out. He's tall and extremely muscular, with an absolute flood of black hair. He's wearing a tacky red suit and tinted sunglasses, and he's carrying a small laser pistol. Apart from the weapon, he looks like he should be on a cheap stage in Vegas with a couple of tigers.

He whips off his sunglasses and fixes She-Hulk with a steely glare. "I said stand down."

Make a focus test. Roll one die, and add your **CONCENTRATION** to it. If your concentration is negative, it will lower your total.

Get 5 or more: turn to **81**.

4 or less: turn to **196**.

102

It's Jen who makes the breakthrough discovery, examining some of the machinery embedded in the arch. "They were *farming* that thing." She sounds appalled. "Little pieces of it were being constantly siphoned off, spun into incredibly thin strands, and coated with something. There's a reservoir of them here." She pats the side of the arch. "They look like spools of ultra-fine wire."

"Like in circuitry?" you ask.

"Very much so."

Ugh. Abomination circuits? "That's unsettling."

"Yeah … you want some?"

Do you? You may take the [Abomination Wire] if you like.

To check out the computer systems, turn to **116**.

Otherwise, to retrace your steps back to Earth and go meet Ruby, turn to **21**.

103

She-Hulk frowns. "I don't know about this. I haven't seen much here to make me seriously doubt the official version of events. I'd love to think she's changed, but it's not hard to imagine Ruby killing the guy in a fit of anger and deciding on a hyper-elaborate excuse. I do truly hate being manipulated."

Take **+1 POWER**.

"We need to know more," she continues. "For now, we keep digging. We definitely need to look into the victim. Maybe he was stringing Ruby along and pushed her too far? I have addresses for the victim's home and for his place of work up in the hills. Where do you think we should start tomorrow?"

"Let's see what he had at home." Turn to **185**.

"His office might be interesting." Turn to **191**.

104

Jen snatches the dumbbell out of the air, and with the slightest suggestion of effort, crumples it into a big, lumpy ball. She drops the ball at her feet and arches one eyebrow. "That was a little rude, don't you think?"

The strongman blinks. "Um. Yeah. Maybe?"

Jen nods encouragingly. "Do you really want to hurt me?"

He thinks about it, which obviously takes some effort. "Well. No. But…"

"But the Ringmaster set you to guard this door. And you have done. It's very impressive."

He looks at the crumpled dumbbell. "Yeah," he says. "Okay. Fine." He heads over to a weight bench, hefts the biggest weight, and starts lifting.

Take **+1 CHARM**.

Jen looks at him for a moment. "Okay," she says. "Right. From here, we can go through to the home theater or the casino. Which do you like the sound of?"

"The theater." Turn to **258**.

"The casino." Turn to **161**.

105

If you have a white ball, your bag is not the bag with two black balls. You've pulled out a white ball, so either your bag contains a white ball or a black ball. Unfortunately, if you have the "black and white" bag, you only end up in this version of reality 50% of the time, but if you have the "two whites" bag, you end up here 100% of the time. That means it's twice as likely that you're currently holding the "two whites" bag than the "black and white" bag – and so the actual probability of getting a second white ball is two thirds. Probability is often counter-intuitive. There, wasn't that fun?

There's a rude buzzer noise from beneath the statue. Take **+1 {WATCHED}**. A section of the terracotta wall shifts color to reveal a pair of doors onwards. They have plaques this time. One says *Temple*, and the other *Pool*.

For the temple, turn to **166**.

For the pool, turn to **62**.

106

Despite Chtylok's best efforts to shake them off, She-Hulk and the Thing are still holding on to the sides of its head like a pair of angry novelty headphones. Its shoulders seem too massively over-muscled to allow it to reach up and pluck them off. The heroes are smashing at the side of its head, trying to strike at the monster's crazed red eyes.

Make a blinding test. Roll two dice, add your **POWER** and **CONCENTRATION**, and subtract your **{WOBBLY}**.

On an 18 or more: turn to **139**.

17 or less: turn to **22**.

107

You need to get close to the airlock door to really see through the porthole. On the other side, there's a small antechamber, metal-walled, and empty apart from another control panel like the one on this side of the door, and a pair of what looks like space suit helmets hanging from pegs on the wall. There are no suits to go with them, however, and they don't seem to have seals at the bottom.

You press the big button, and the door whooshes open. If you'd like the [Odd Helmets], they take up one slot in your inventory for the pair. Looking through the door inside the antechamber, you see another relatively normal-looking corridor ahead. There's no sign of vacuum, an isolation ward, or anything else that might demand an airlock.

She-Hulk looks at you expectantly.

To go through the airlock, turn to **68**.

To head back to the middle of the lab, turn to **184**.

108

She-Hulk and Chtylok separate and circle each other warily. Even hunched over, the monster is still fifteen feet tall. It has apparently realized that she's not just some tasty raisin to devour, but it doesn't seem harmed. Jen darts forward, aiming to dash between its towering legs. It kicks out at her, and connects with a horrible meaty thud. She's flung clear out of the main arena to crunch painfully into the stone seats. Take +1 {WOBBLY}.

Arcade cackles in delight.

She-Hulk stands back up, holding a very solid-looking stone bench that could probably seat six. She takes a moment to aim, then hurls it Chtylok so ferociously that it blurs through the air.

Make an impromptu missile test. Roll one die, add your **CONCENTRATION**, and subtract your {WOBBLY}.

On an 11 or more: turn to **151**.

10 or less: turn to **289**.

109

There's a cabinet on one wall that reminds you of something. It takes you a moment to place it, but then you realize – you saw it in one of Bright's notes, flagged up as a security device whose manufacturers were unusually obscure. You open the cabinet, and press the switch that Bright's notes described as *Off*.

Take +1 {DRONED} and +1 {NOBBLED}.

A wall panel slides up into the ceiling to reveal a long, sterile-looking white corridor lit by flickering strip-lights. ACHIEVEMENT: *Cosmic Tunnel*.

"Nice," She-Hulk says. "This has to be better than a courtyard filled with high-speed murder-drones." She thinks about that for a moment. "Better let me go first though, yeah?"

When she gets to the far end of the corridor without any problems, you follow. There's a side door about three quarters of the way along, and another door at the far end. By the far door is a [Security Pass] that you may take with you.

"We're well into the main building here," She-Hulk says. "That first door comes out somewhere near the building's entrance, but this one is definitely deeper."

To take the first door, turn to **300**.

To try the deeper door, Turn to **39**.

110

"Go for the neck!" you shout.

The robot actually flinches a little, and raises its laser-cutter protectively. Take **+1 CONCENTRATION**.

She-Hulk grins ferociously and leaps up onto the thing, landing on its shoulders to grab it firmly by the head. It reels around, gun-ports firing uselessly, as she starts to twist.

Make a rage check. Roll one die and add your **POWER**. If the total is 6 or less, decapitating the robot takes a whole half a minute longer than you hoped. Grrr! Take **-1 POWER**.

Jen strains, and the robot's head rips off. Its body freezes, then topples. ACHIEVEMENT: *Terminator Too.*

To examine the broken robot, turn to **221**.

To check out the garden, turn to **250**.

111

Kangaroo flies back through the wall into the room behind with an almighty crash. You distinctly hear a slightly muffled "Crikey!" She-Hulk darts in there, and a moment later she reappears, flying through the air with Kangaroo held out in front of her, upside down. They land in the middle of the street in a perfect, if savage, piledriver. Make a note of the number 88.

Kangaroo groans and collapses. She-Hulk rips his metal tail off, pulls out several feet of stout wiring from inside it, and trusses him up like a roast.

If you've noted three numbers now, add them up and head over to that entry.

Otherwise, you can let She-Hulk take a breath, or start in on interrogating Kangaroo.

For a breather, turn to **124**.

To talk to the Australian, turn to **168**.

112

Jen walks up to the guards, an expression of mild curiosity on her face, and openly studies the main man and his equipment. He ignores her for a few seconds, then he breaks. "What?" he demands, his voice a menacing growl.

She smiles at him. "I was wondering why you were carrying blatantly illegal weaponry in violation of state criminal law."

"What?" he repeats, but this time he sounds just a touch uncertain. His friends look unhappy.

"Cabinet Holdings, the company running this Expo, does not have any sort of assault weapon exemption from the Department of Justice, let alone one for advanced tech like that. I checked. That's a felony crime with a sentence of up to four years for a first offence. You seem remarkably calm for a man heading to prison. Or is that *back* to prison?"

"Who the hell are you, lady?"

"Oh, I'm just a crusading lawyer who *hates* gun violations," Jen says sweetly.

"Look, uh, you want something, right? What do you want?"

"In."

The men share a look, reach a decision. "Right away, ma'am."

The one nearest the door swipes a card, and it opens. You walk through into a small stretch of beige corridor. There are three frosted glass doors at the other end, one directly ahead and the other two set in the walls opposite each other. One is red, one is green, and one is blue.

"I've got a bad feeling about this," Jen says. "What's your favorite color?"

"Red." Turn to **194**.

"Green." Turn to **178**.

"Blue." Turn to **298**.

113

Tekeli Industries occupies an entire block in Mountain View. There are tall gray stone walls with regular security cameras, broken only by a single gatehouse. Behind the barred gate, you can see a traffic island with an ornamental fountain where the road divides into two and heads into some trees. A tall, undistinguished office building lurks behind them.

You make your way through to the guest car park, and

from there to the reception lobby. You sign in as Ruby's minions. Take +1 {SIMPATICO}.

The receptionist actually manages to pretend that athletic green women are a normal part of his day, and verifies your appointment smoothly. Whatever they pay him, he deserves a raise. You are issued lurid green pass-cards that clash nastily with Jen's skin. "Someone will be with you shortly to escort you to Mr Gould's office," he informs you dispassionately. "Please wait over there."

You obediently meander to the couches he indicated. He's not watching you ferociously, but every now and again, he looks over to check. Across the sprawling lobby, past a coffee concession, you see a pair of frosted glass doors with *RESTRICTED* blazing across them, and a card reader, painted red.

"Are we feeling... obedient?" Jen asks.

To wait as instructed, turn to **24**.

To duck into a rest room, turn to **50**.

114

Ruby shrugs. "Fifteen bedrooms, set in forty acres of nicely discreet woodland overlooking the Pacific Ocean. Frankly, it's tasteless – more of an advertising expense than a home. If you don't show off your vulgarity round here, no one takes your company seriously."

"Security systems?" Jen asks.

"Depends who's squatting. You might want to avoid the front door to be safe, but the guest wing and the kitchen have exterior doors too, and the gym opens onto the pool. They're all options. My office is at the heart of the ground floor. That's where you'll find the files. There are several ways into it – look for red lights above sturdy oak doors. Break whatever you need to, of course. It's just stuff."

"I'll try to keep it to a minimum," She-Hulk says drily. "No promises if there's another giant robot, though."

To ask if there's anything she needs, turn to **80**.

To ask about the bail situation, if you haven't already, turn to **30**.

Or to visit the mansion, turn to **209**.

115

She-Hulk punches the robot savagely in the chest. It doesn't even sway back. She curses and jumps back several feet to regroup. Turning to the side, she wrenches one of the wooden benches clean out of the ground. A chunk of concrete sticks to each end, and beneath the wood, you can see some sturdy metalwork. As the robot readies its sword, she steps forward, swinging the bench like it was a baseball bat.

This is a boss fight.

Round one: roll two dice and add your **POWER** and, if you have any, your {TROUBLESOME}. If the total is 13 or more, you win the first round.

Round two: roll two dice and add your **POWER** and, if you have any, your {TROUBLESOME} and your {NOBBLED}. If the total is 14 or more, you win the second round.

Round three: roll two dice and add your **POWER** and, if

you have any, your {TROUBLESOME} and your {NOBBLED}. If the total is 15 or more, you win the third round.

Subtract 1 from the number of rounds you won, and adjust your **POWER** by that much: that could range from **+2** if you won all three, to **-1** if you lost all three.

The bench shatters, and She-Hulk's expression is grim. The robot seems fine. You want to help. Which potential weak-spot are you going to suggest?

"Go for the knee!" Turn to **287**.

"Go for the power core!" Turn to **162**.

116

The computer equipment is live, running all sorts of analysis software. Some of the screens are flagging up errors now that the abomination is goo, but others are still showing various results. It doesn't take too much work to piece the evidence together: the system is running pattern recognition tests. Neither of you know the field well enough to know if the results are impressive. However, you *are* in a deep space lab somewhere outside the galaxy, having seamlessly stepped through some vastly implausible portal, and now sharing a room with the decaying remains of a vast alien horror. It seems safe to assume that Tekeli Industries thinks this is worth the effort.

Jen films some footage of the test results to show to Ruby later. Take +1 {WHEELS WITHIN WHEELS}.

> To examine the arch and the remains of the abomination, turn to **102**.
>
> Otherwise, to retrace your steps back to Earth and go meet Ruby, turn to **21**.

117

Initially, the restricted section is a fairly normal-looking white tiled corridor – wider than usual maybe, and without windows or decoration, but not actually peculiar. Office doors here and there, but you decide not to risk them. As you explore, the corridor changes. After one junction, the lighting shifts to fluorescent floor strips, bright but casting odd shadows toward the ceiling. After another turn, there's a series of a dozen huge metal shutter-doors, ten yards apart. Just how big is this complex?

There has been quiet conversation and other sounds behind each door you've passed so far. Despite this, you've not seen another living soul. It's eerie.

"It's cheap, more like," She-Hulk mutters.

Leading off from another junction, the corridor narrows, and the walls become brushed steel. You come to a pair of glass doors, and despite the murmurings that you can clearly hear coming from them, you can see that both rooms are empty of people. One of the rooms looks like a lab of some sort. The other one is smallish, and appears to hold some sort of big, free-standing glowing panel.

"These rooms look empty," Jen says. "Let's investigate. Which one do you prefer?"

"The laboratory." Turn to **184**.

"The room with the glow." Turn to **276**.

118

She-Hulk goes over to Marion, the judge's sister, and spends some time reassuring her. With some gentle, patient questioning, you learn that she was treated comparatively well. The Black Fox, apparently, was as much the gentleman with her as he was during your brief encounter. Both he and Kangaroo claimed that she was to be released on Monday.

"They told me that my sister's obedience wouldn't matter any more, and the things I knew wouldn't be a problem," Marion explains. "Kangaroo definitely believed it. He lies as convincingly as a six year-old. Fox, no idea either way, but he certainly claimed it was true."

Take +1 {WHEELS WITHIN WHEELS}.

To get Marion back to the judge, turn to **182**.

To call Ruby and fill her in, turn to **188**.

Taking careful hold of you, She-Hulk gathers herself at the base of the wall, then jumps. There's a dizzying *whoosh* before the pair of you land on top of the wall, which you discover is actually several feet thick.

Loud clicking alerts you to the presence of experimental-looking weapons turrets either side of you along the wall. One is ten feet away on the left, the other about thirty feet to the right. They swivel to face you, and you immediately fling yourself flat on the wall-top.

She-Hulk stands over you protectively, and rips out a big chunk of stone from the wall.

This is a fight. Round one: roll two dice and add your **POWER**. If the total is 10 or more, you win the first round.

Round two: roll two dice and add your **POWER**. If the total is 10 or more, you win the second round.

She-Hulk takes out both turrets while keeping the fire trained on her either way, but if you won both rounds, take **+1 POWER**.

Once the turrets are smashed, she looks thoughtfully at the paved surface that runs along the top of the wall. "This wall might not be entirely solid," she says.

To investigate the walls thoroughly, turn to **47**.

To go down to the courtyard, turn to **202**.

120

As Jen approaches, Walrus's hammer catches her square on the jaw. She staggers back several feet, looking stunned and outraged. She shakes her head to clear it, but he's already there, swinging again, to take her in the ribs this time. She responds with a savage head-butt which pushes him back a pace. He growls and brings the hammer arcing down in a brutal overhead blow.

This is a tough fight.

Round one: roll two dice, add your **POWER**, and subtract your {**PENALTY**}. If the total is 12 or more, you win the first round.

Round two: roll two dice, add your **POWER**, and subtract your {**PENALTY**}. If the total is 13 or more, you win the second round.

Round three: roll two dice, add your **POWER**, and subtract your {**PENALTY**}. For this round, if you have [**Spiked Knuckles**], add 2 to your total. If the total is 12 or more, you win the third round.

If you won at least two rounds, turn to **284**.

If you won one round, turn to **91**.

If you lost all three, turn to **213**.

121

Jen's screams of pain are fading to whimpers, and her struggles are becoming weaker. The abomination obviously feels she's taken care of, because it surges forward, faster than you thought possible. Moments later, it's reaching for you with an army of pseudopods. They latch on like metal chains. You endure a moment of shrieking red agony, and then everything just… stops.

ACHIEVEMENT: *Just Like a Toothpaste Tube.*

The end.

122

A rogue flurry of chain gun bullets forces you to duck behind a couch for several seconds. When you peek back up, Ruby is closing on Big Wheel, lashing out toward his weapons systems with spikes of furious energy. Oort is a blur, zipping around the room so quickly that you can barely see him. Plasma blasts shoot out at She-Hulk from all angles; she ducks and weaves as she attempts to predict his movements enough to land a solid blow.

This is a tricky fight.

Round one: roll two dice and add your **POWER** and **CHARM** to factor in Ruby's help. If the total is 14 or more, you win the first round.

Round two: roll two dice and add your **POWER** and **CHARM** to factor in Ruby's help. If the total is 14 or more, you win the second round.

If you win at least one round: turn to **40**.

If you lose both rounds: turn to **295**.

123

Jen waits until the woman on the desk has a moment, then goes over to her with a self-deprecating smile. "Hey there. I'm here to meet my client for the first time in a long while. Thursday Rubinstein. She's been a bit of a terror in the past. Any idea what I'm in for here?"

The lady lights up. "Wow! She-Hulk! You're representing Dr R? Wow! Well, she's a delight. Super polite, super cooperative, and since she's been here, bad behavior in her pod has dropped to absolutely nothing. Like, really, totally zero. No one has seen anything like it. Our guys love her."

"Wow," Jen echoes. "That's good to hear." She looks slightly troubled, though. "Thanks for your time."

"Any time," the lady says.

To go in and wait, turn to **59**.

To freshen up first, turn to **38**.

124

You stand back up properly and dust some of the grit off your knees, while She-Hulk tidies herself up a little and takes a moment to refocus.

If any of your **POWER**, **CHARM**, or **CONCENTRATION** are less than 3, set them to 3 now.

To head up into the hotel, turn to **31**.

To interrogate Kangaroo first, turn to **168**.

125

Jen snatches the dumbbell out of the air and tosses it straight back without thinking. It smacks Bruto in the stomach, and he drops like someone cut his strings. She dashes over to him and checks him over. "Just dazed, the poor silly man," she says with evident relief. "I hope I didn't do any serious damage. I'll call an ambulance for him once it's safe for them to approach."

Take +1 **POWER** and +1 {INTENSITY}.

"For now, we need to press on," she says. "From here, we can go through to the home theater or the casino. Which do you like the sound of?"

"The theater." Turn to **258**.

"The casino." Turn to **161**.

126

Brandishing the [Onyx Pass-card], you walk over to the restricted section. No one shouts out to stop you or otherwise gives any sign of alarm. You look around, and press the card against the reader.

Make a timing test. Roll one die, and add your **CONCENTRATION**.

Get 5 or more: turn to **117**.

4 or less: turn to **232**.

127

The library you find yourselves in is spacious, and very well stocked with textbooks and journals on a wide range of scientific and technical subjects. Programming and electronic engineering are particularly well-represented. There's also a wall devoted to science fiction novels. There are no people around.

Do you have a [Security Pass]? If you do, skip this paragraph. If not, alas, there is a loud bleep from the far wall, and a noise that sounds worryingly like something charging up. She-Hulk just has time to step in front of you before a bright bolt of plasma crackles across the room. Make a dodge test. Roll one die and add your **POWER**. If the total is 8 or less, the bolt hits her painfully in the neck, so take **-1 POWER** and the ACHIEVEMENT: *That Tickles.*

Now, there's a large exit door with a push-bar leading out of the library halfway along the wall ahead of you, but there's also a smaller doorway that looks like it leads to a reading room.

If you want to take the exit, turn to **206**.

If you'd rather try the reading room, turn to **12**.

128

The Sixth District courthouse in San José looks like a mid-range commuter hotel. You follow Jen in and past security, ignoring the nervous stares, and the pair of you cut a swathe through the building to Judge Hirst's chambers. As you walk in, the secretary visibly winces, then straightens up. "I'm afraid the Judge is not available, Miss Walters."

Jen arches an eyebrow, but doesn't vary her pace. "She's clearly expecting me, I'd say."

A flash of panic crosses the secretary's face. "No, I'm afraid she's not here."

"Don't be afraid," Jen says, only a little menacingly. She yanks the Judge's door open with a loud crack as the lock breaks, and keeps walking. "Oopsie."

The judge is standing up behind her desk, looking alarmed.

"I'll pay for the accidental damage, of course. Hello, Judge Hirst. We need a word." She ushers you in and pulls the ruined door closed behind her. "Firm or friendly, do you think?" she asks quietly.

Beneath the obvious fear, the judge is a pleasant-looking African-American woman in her fifties with intelligent eyes and some smile-lines.

"Firm." Turn to **169**.

"Friendly." Turn to **70**.

129

There's a brief flurry of action, tough to follow in the dim attic. A huge metal spike slams into a wall near you with a *sproing*. "Oof," Spellcheck groans, and collapses.

She-Hulk looks down at him. "Wow. Glass jaw." She gives him a nudge with one foot. "Yep, he's out."

Take +1 {REASONABLE DOUBT}.

The pair of you look around the attic. At the back of the space, you find a huge corkboard pinned with maps, photographs, scraps of newspaper article, and a dazzling web of red thread connecting it all. A large Thurstech logo is near the heart of the chaos. You start photographing everything carefully.

Take +1 {MURDERBOARD}.

With Spellcheck tied up and stashed on the porch, and the police anonymously called to come and pick him up, you move on.

"Well, do you think we have enough to go on, or would you rather search Bright's workplace?" She-Hulk asks you.

"We've got enough." Turn to **252**.

"Better safe than sorry." Turn to **191**.

130

The hotel is a crumbling heap on a decaying street in a deeply poor neighborhood. It's not possible to exactly speed recklessly given the disastrous state of the road surface, but the car sweeps up to the sagging front doors, and the pair of you pile out before the motor has stopped ticking.

You're halfway up the steps when you hear a crash above you, and a big, muscular man comes dropping down from the third floor in a cloud of glass. He lands on the pavement as you both turn around, Jen stepping in front of you. The man is unshaven, with short, untidy hair, and a can of beer in one hand. He's wearing some sort of tawny body and leg armor, with a long chunky tail out the back.

"G'day, Red," he says casually, but his attempt at nonchalance is spoiled when he notices the beer, swears, drops it, tries to kick the can aside, and misses. "Flaming Nora," he mutters.

"Hello, Brian," She-Hulk says. "I don't suppose we can have the judge's sister back peacefully, can we?"

"Strewth, mate, Buckley's chance," he replies, almost incomprehensibly.

He makes a sudden lunge, trying to grab Jen's suit. He's surprisingly fast. Make a dodge test. Roll one die and add your Power.

Get a total of 9 or more: turn to **2**.

8 or less: turn to **274**.

131

You follow She-Hulk past the restricted doors and into a stretch of blandly corporate corridor. She turns into a side-passage and about halfway down stops near a meeting room. After opening the door and peeking in, she waves you inside. "The far wall should back onto something in the restricted zone, unless the layout is way screwier than I think. We're going through."

Ah. "Right."

"Check the corridor."

You look out quickly. "No one visible."

A deep tearing noise rumbles through the room as soon as you close the door. Take +1 {WAVES} and +1 {WEIRD VIBES} as a strange sensation washes over and through you. In moments, Jen has ripped a big section of dividing wall down.

Did you attract attention? Make a timing test. Roll one die and add your **POWER**.

9 or more: turn to **117**.

8 or less: Turn to **232**.

132

"Theories? Nothing good. It's obviously not you, since you're right here and Reed's wand isn't going insane. Bruce is supposed to be in Patagonia or something…"

"He is," Jen says. "He's found some promising steppe beetle with exciting possibilities or something."

"Steppe beetles. Right. Amadeus is in Manila, Rick's off finding himself in Prague, Thad is cured, and Skaar is back haunting the Pyrenees. So whoever or whatever it is, it's bad news."

To ask about the sensor data, turn to **100**.

To ask what he knows about the Expo, turn to **142**.

To suggest working together, turn to **198**.

133

Unsurprisingly, Ruby's secure office has impressive internet and telecommunications facilities. You and Jen go to work on the case, getting hold of all the information that's out there. Within a half hour, it's obvious that Ruby's arrest stinks. She was pulled in within twenty minutes of the murder and charged before she was even properly interviewed. It's not quite illegal, but it's beyond the point of shoddy. There's no way it will hold up, and whoever arranged it has to know that.

The bail application was similarly perfunctory. Her regular company attorney applied for bail, and was rejected summarily. The rejection was issued by a member of the Sixth Appellate Circuit, one Judge Hirst.

"It's not normal for Appeals Judges to get bail applications," you say. "It should be the day's Criminal Duty Judge."

Jen nods. "You know where the Sixth Circuit Court is?"

"Sure, downtown San José. I've been there once or twice."

"Great. We need a little chat with Judge Hirst."

To head back to San José, turn to **128**.

To bring Ruby up to date, turn to **281**.

134

You tap at the keyboard for a while, but nothing happens. The correct answer to the puzzle is actually 117 – calculate terms in brackets, then calculate multiplications and divisions, and only then calculate additions and subtractions.

"Worth a shot," Jen says, and presses the intercom button with a faint shrug.

"Yes?" The voice crackling through the speaker is brisk and female, businesslike.

"Jennifer Walters, attorney-at-law. May I speak with someone in charge?"

There's a long silence. "It's your funeral," the voice says finally. "I'm upstairs, if you make it."

How... encouraging.

"Thank you, ma'am," Jen says. "We'll be there shortly."

"We'll see." The door buzzes, and you enter a corridor with polished wooden floors and off-white walls, decorated sparsely with paintings of futuristic cityscapes. It all looks suspiciously normal. There are simple wooden doors at each end of the corridor with nothing much to distinguish them, except that there's a faint draft of fresh air coming from the door to the right.

She-Hulk looks at you expectantly.

"Let's go left." Turn to **127**.

"Let's go right." Turn to **206**.

135

She-Hulk and Kangaroo collide in mid-air. While the big Australian has the body mass, his momentum is no match for the power behind Jen's leap. She forces him onto a second floor balcony, landing comfortably while he sprawls. Take **+1 POWER** and remember the number 92.

Kangaroo flails and springs to his feet, right into She-Hulk's foot.

Make a kick test. Roll one die, add your **POWER**, and subtract your {FLAT-FOOTED}, if any.

8 or more: Turn to **111**.

7 or less: Turn to **72**.

136

You suggest ripping the paintings down to Jen, who smiles. "Yes, let's."

Do you have a [Claw Glove]? That would make this all much easier – you can skip past the next paragraph.

She-Hulk lays into the paintings. You were expecting them to be well-disguised video screens, but they not, they're some sort of fabric reinforced with a thin layer of a strong substrate that contains internal electronics, and the frames are very firmly set into the wall. It takes several minutes to rip everything down. Take **+1** {WATCHED}.

With the paintings shredded, you see a pair of doors leading onwards. They have plaques this time. One says *Temple*, and the other says *Pool*.

For the temple, turn to **166**.

For the pool, turn to **62**.

137

The spa area looks like the lobby of any luxury service establishment, with an impressive reception desk, stylish waiting chairs, healthy plants, and a selection of glossy magazines. Frosted glass doors lead deeper into the place.

More importantly, across the room, you see a sturdy looking oak door with a red light above it, and a big keypad to one side. The entry to the secure suite. You head over there. Jen tries the code Ruby gave her, but unsurprisingly it doesn't work.

This is a puzzle! Look at the following numbers: *27, 49, 67, 125, 169.*

One of them is unlike the others, an odd one out. Turn to that entry, and if the first words you see are not "This is the odd one out!", turn to **195**.

Alternatively, you can take a penalty and bypass the puzzle by turning to **29**.

138

"He was electrocuted while lifting weights in the gym here. There was a complicated contraption set up to make contact with live wires if he got the barbell up to a certain height. It seems ridiculous, really. But it killed him anyway."

Do you have {**NOT JUST A NUMBER**} of 1? If so, Jen asks about Sturm's interest in the six companies, and whether it's possible Ruby might have been involved. Exie thinks it's wildly unlikely, and says that Sturm and Ruby were on good terms. Take **+2 {REASONABLE DOUBT}**.

To ask about Sturm as a person, turn to **296**.

To go visit Ruby in jail finally, turn to **89**.

139

"KHAAAW!!" With a howl of fury, Chtylok goes absolutely berserk. You cower in terror as the monster thrashes around in a wild frenzy. She-Hulk and the Thing take cover across the arena, battered and exhausted. It lashes out at the arena itself, bringing whole sections crashing down upon itself. From the noises coming from further away, the monster has actually brought a whole chunk of this conference center down. Take +1 {WAVES}.

Eventually the monster slowly winds down, shaking its head again and again. Then to your astonishment, it lies down, curls up, and starts snoring.

"It really is a chicken," the Thing says. "It can't see anything, so it must be time to sleep. I can keep this ugly baby under wraps until Reed gets here. Go stop that little weasel Arcade."

What is your {WHEELS WITHIN WHEELS} score?

    4 or more: turn to **244**.
    3 or less: turn to **290**.

140

The bench smacks Chtylok in the side of the head, making the monster stumble and blink for a couple of seconds. She-Hulk attempts to press the advantage, but it recovers too quickly. As the fight progresses, neither seems able to do much lasting damage to the other. If the creature could get a truly solid blow in, Jen might be in serious trouble. Arcade continually yammers on from the sidelines like a sports commentator, but you're ignoring him.

There's a loud crunch just a short distance behind you, and you whip round to see the Thing burst through the arena wall. He looks at the fight, nods to you, then glances at a watch. "Yeah, that's the signal. I made it in …53 seconds. Not bad. Anything I need to know so far, friend?"

Is that all? It feels like the fight's been going for ages. "Arcade seemed to use a high-pitched sound to set it off," you say.

You both wince as She-Hulk is hammered into the arena wall again.

"Got it," the Thing says. He sprints into the fray, and She-Hulk seizes Chtylok's momentary distraction to jump up like a rocket and punch it in the beak. She lands back down as it staggers, and exchanges a few words with the Thing.

She-Hulk grabs the Thing, and jumps. A moment later, they're clinging to the feathers either side of Chtylok's head.

"*Kraw!*" it roars.

Make a clobbering test for Jen and Ben. Roll two dice, add your **POWER** twice, then subtract your {**WOBBLY**} once.

  20 or more: turn to **218**.

  19 or less: turn to **139**.

141

The guard shrugs. "You can leave it here. I'll make sure it gets to him."

Jen shakes her head. "No can do. Ms Rubinstein needs us to deliver this to Mr Gould personally."

"Not my problem."

She rolls her eyes, and fishes out a fifty from her purse, which she lets him see. "There's usually no problem."

He wavers for a moment, then shrugs again. "Fine." He produces a couple of lurid green swipe-cards and takes the cash. You feel a momentary pressure on the back of your neck, as if someone was staring at you, but it vanishes as swiftly as it comes. Take **-1 CHARM** and **+1 {WEIRD VIBES}**.

You make your way from visitor parking to the sprawling lobby, passes prominently displayed. There's a lot of security around, but no one calls you out. Past a coffee concession, you spot a large pair of frosted glass doors with *RESTRICTED* stenciled across them. And there's a card reader next to them, colored red. As you look, a short-haired person in a pinstriped suit walks up and swipes a bright red card. The doors open, revealing a long corridor. The worker bustles through impatiently, then the doors close behind them. No one else appears to pay any notice.

"We could try to follow someone through," Jen says. "Or we could just make our own entrance."

"Let's try to slip in." Turn to **171**.

"Let's be direct." Turn to **131**.

142

"I heard a few things," he says. "There's new management, and the staff hate it. The previous company went bust, and there were a couple of accidents. It's got a huge game hall devoted to parting kids from their money, and a smaller consumer electronics hall for techies to spend their company cash in. The restaurant is terrible and way too expensive, and so is the built-in hotel. It's loud and cramped and smelly in there. That's about it."

"I can hardly wait," Jen says.

The Thing snorts. "I'm surprised you're not in there already."

To ask if Ben has any theories, turn to **132**.

To ask about the sensor data, turn to **100**.

To suggest working together, turn to **198**.

143

Alas, "Drop" is not the word closest in meaning to the other four. If you have both {MURDERBOARD} and {FILES} of 1, return immediately to **252** and try again.

If not, you do your best to put together the pieces you have, but it's tangled. Bright was very scared, that much is obvious. He's tracked more than a hundred deaths in the last three months that are clustered around six companies. These include both Thurstech and Omni and Grey.

The root cause of his concern however seems to be the recent death of a famous tech visionary, Sturm Vanguard.

Bright was definitely onto something. Vanguard was interested in the six companies before his death seemed to kick off all the others. All six CEOs, including Ruby, had meetings at his sprawling personal compound.

One note of Bright's highlights the identity of a sandwich truck that makes deliveries to the compound every day, along with its schedule. Set {FOOD TRUCK} to 1.

To dig deeper into the six companies, turn to **233**.

To research Vanguard a bit further, turn to **238**.

144

"That might work, I guess," Jen says. "Grab something from the inventory and wave it around menacingly."

You blink. "The what?"

"Your bag. Anything. Quickly!"

Choose an object from your inventory to threaten Bi-Beast with. If you aren't carrying anything better, you can use your mobile phone, which doesn't take an inventory slot.

"Do you know what my companion is holding?" Jen asks, her voice full of confidence.

Bi-Beast looks at you. One face says, "We do not care," at the same time as the other declares, "We demand information."

"One of you is a fool," Jen says.

The faces snarl. "Do not speak so of my other," they both say. The android stops approaching, and you hear the faces start bickering quietly.

"My companion holds the Quantum Tesseract. It is the pinnacle of human science, our newest weapon – and it is your destruction."

Make an intimidation test. Roll one die and add your Charm, and if you are holding up either the [Mysterious Skull], the [Glop], the [Glowing Pearl], or the [Evil Cowbell], add +3.

Get a 10 or more: turn to **174**.

9 or less: turn to **49**.

145

The pack are dealt with, and you have a second or two to feel good about that before a loud buzzer sounds, and all the monitors in the room click on to show an intense pair of eyes. "Stand down, She-Hulk," a voice says, echoing from all around you.

Make a luck roll. Roll one die. If you have a [Squirmy Owlet], add 3.

On a 4 or more: nothing happens.

3 or less: Whatever your {COOL} is, subtract that many points from your stats in any combination you choose. You can't go below 0 here, and hitting 0 in a stat does not have any immediate bad effects.

"Yeah, right," She-Hulk murmurs. She sounds offended.

An office door opens at the back of the room, and a man comes out. He's tall and extremely muscular, with an absolute flood of black hair. He's wearing a cheap red suit and tinted sunglasses, and he's carrying a small laser pistol.

Apart from the weapon, he looks like he should be on a stage in Vegas with a couple of tigers.

He whips off his sunglasses and fixes She-Hulk with a steely glare. "I said stand down."

Make a focus test. Roll one die, and add your **CONCENTRATION** to it.

Get a 5 or more: turn to **81**.

4 or less: turn to **196**.

146

She-Hulk and Chtylok collide in mid-air. The beast must weigh several tons, but She-Hulk's leap has so much force behind it that as the two impact, they drop to the sand together. She's swinging savage punches at the beast as they land, but it completely ignores them to grab her by the head and fling her straight into the stone arena wall as if she was a rag-doll.

She groans and slides down to the sand, but she's already rolling away. A moment later, Chtylok slams a huge fist down where she was just lying. She flips herself to her feet, grabs a hoofed leg, and tries to wrench it.

With another shattering "*Kraw!*", the beast aims a brutal peck at her head.

This is a fierce fight.

Round one: roll two dice, add your **POWER**, and subtract your {**WOBBLY**}. If the total is 12 or more, you win the first round.

Round two: roll two dice, add your **POWER**, and subtract

your {WOBBLY}. If the total is 13 or more, you win the second round.

If you won either round, turn to **245**.

If you lost both rounds, turn to **108**.

147

This is a textbook example of an interior designer's idea of a single young man's lounge. There are arty coffee table books arrayed on the arty coffee table, a thick shag-pile carpet, tastefully expensive sofas and love-seats, safely abstract paintings, mood lighting, and even a well-stocked wine bar. A suave room, for a sophisticated seducer.

Two marble busts on short stone columns seem like a very odd addition, however. Roman emperors, you'd guess. Was that a scraping noise from one of them? Take **+1 CONCENTRATION**.

"Careful," you say quickly.

As She-Hulk looks round, the column bases open and several angry snakes come out hissing. You don't recognize the species. Take **+1 {REASONABLE DOUBT}**.

This is an easy fight. Roll two dice and add your **POWER**. If the total is 8 or more, you win the only round without any trouble.

If you lost, one of the snakes darts past She-Hulk to chomp you on the ankle. It stings a little. Take **+1 {BITTEN}**. Surely it's fine – you know all the dangerously poisonous local snake species. You think.

With all the snakes dispatched, the room looks considerably less pristine.

"Everything OK?" Jen asks.

"Absolutely."

"Great. Where next?"

To check out the kitchen, turn to **156**.

To search the home office, turn to **25**.

148

Jen looks at Teena doubtfully, but she nods, and smiles pleasantly. "I prefer Jen, Mary. I know you're very dangerous in a fight, but I really am not your enemy here. I'm not here for the Circus at all. Strong women need to stick together, not let scrawny men goad us into harming each other. How about I tell the Ringmaster you beat me good and proper, but I managed to escape when your back was turned?"

Teena gives that some thought.

Make a persuasion test. Roll one die, and add your **CHARM** to it.

On a score of 7 or more: Teena nods. "Okay, Jen." She seems to enjoy using the name. "Girls together, huh? Let's try it." She retreats into the kitchens. Take **+1 CHARM**.

6 or less: Teena just growls, backs up two feet, and begins

a lumbering charge, massive ring-laden fists ready to fly. Jen steps forward, one arm out, and catches Teena by the top of the head. The big woman grunts, but she can't even get close enough to punch. She pushes harder, and Jen twists out of the way, using the woman's own weight to send her flying out the door. After twenty feet, Teena slows for a moment, then just keeps on going, off into the grounds.

Jen shrugs. "According to the floorplan, the kitchens lead on to the parlor and the dining room," she says. "Which way?"

"How about the parlor?" Turn to **292**.

"Let's try the dining room." Turn to **3**.

149

Alas, "Establish" is not the word closest in meaning to the other four. If you have both {MURDERBOARD} and {FILES} of 1, you may return to **252** and try again now.

If not, you do your best to put together the pieces you have, but it's tangled. Bright was very scared, that much is obvious. He's tracked more than a hundred deaths in the last three months that are clustered around six companies. These include both Thurstech and Omni and Grey. The root cause of his concern however seems to be the recent death of a famous tech visionary, Sturm Vanguard. At first Bright's notes read like mad rambling, but it quickly becomes clear that he was onto something. Vanguard was interested in the six companies before his death. All six CEOs, including Ruby, had meetings at his sprawling personal compound.

One note of Bright's highlights the source of the compound's daily food deliveries, along with its schedule. Set {DELIVERY PATTERNS} to 1.

To dig deeper into the six companies, turn to **233**.

To research Vanguard a bit further, turn to **238**.

150

You've never liked LA. It sprawls on endlessly, a bland snarl of traffic jams and car fumes punctuated by overpriced strip malls. ElectroCon is being held at a vast conference center in the suburban wilds to the west of Anaheim and north of the Long Beach airport. You head down to the area on Friday night. After a seriously overpriced night in an indifferent hotel staffed by underpaid exhaustion-zombies, you and Jen get to the venue not too long after it opens.

It's absolutely thronged with excitable people, many of them in outlandish costumes. There's a contingent of professional types in suits too, but they're well outnumbered by the consumer crowd. Given the colorful ads plastering surrounding apartment blocks and hanging from every available surface, this is plainly a big event on the computer gaming calendar. For once, no one even gives She-Hulk a second glance.

You're making your way to the main entrance when Jen starts beaming, and beelines for a big guy dressed for New York City rainstorms. He's got his head buried in a broadsheet newspaper.

"Ben!"

The guy looks up, and you recognize his broken-rock complexion immediately: Ben Grimm, the Thing. He grins hugely. "Jen? Hey you! Are you a sight for sore eyes – what are you doing in this dump?"

To let Jen and the Thing catch up, turn to **254**.

To suggest she tells him about the mission, turn to **275**.

151

The bench smacks Chtylok in the thigh. It barely stumbles. As the fight progresses, neither seems able to do much lasting damage to the other, but if the creature gets a solid blow in, She-Hulk might be in serious trouble.

Arcade continually yammers on from the sidelines like a sports commentator, but you're ignoring him.

There's a loud crunch just a short distance behind you, and you whip round to see the Thing burst through the arena wall. He looks at the fight, nods to you, then glances at a watch. "Yeah, that's the signal. I made it in … 53 seconds. Not bad. Anything I need to know so far, friend?"

Is that all? It feels like the fight's been going for ages. "It's incredibly strong, but it's dumb and slow," you remark. You both wince as She-Hulk is hammered into the arena wall again.

"Got it," the Thing says. He sprints into the fray, and exchanges a few words with She-Hulk who grabs him, and jumps. A moment later, they're clinging to the feathers either side of Chtylok's head.

"*Kraw!*" it screeches.

Make a clobbering test for Jen and Ben. Roll two dice, add your **POWER** twice, then subtract your {WOBBLY} just the once.

Get a 20 or more: turn to **106**.

19 or less: turn to **265**.

152

You walk into the visitor's lodge. A smiling receptionist is sitting behind a long pine counter. Large photographic prints of hilly forest landscapes festoon the walls. A tall, balding man with a hangdog face and a nice suit is standing in front of the counter.

As you enter, he takes a step forward and raises a hand in greeting. "Ken Winton, Omni and Grey. Welcome. We are one. How may I help today?"

Jen turns to you. "Should I go lawyerly or play nice?" she whispers to you.

"Lawyerly." Turn to **48**.

"Nice." Turn to **83**.

153

It takes a bit of digging around online, but soon the two of you get an idea of precisely how fortified the Vanguard compound could be. The company has several very quiet contracts with the Pentagon, all linked to futuristic warfare solutions – primarily unmanned autonomous vehicles of all sizes and functions, but also robots, personal enhancement technologies, deep imaging, and even laser weaponry. Take **+1 {SECURE}**.

The Vanguard compound has been locked down since Sturm's death. Very few people have been seen going in or coming out, which drove the press mad to start with. They seem to have lost interest, but local sources still talk about how insular the place has become. It certainly used to be a very open site, and the local town of Pacific Bay has been suffering financially, having come to depend on lively business from the compound. It's very curious.

To research Sturm Vanguard further, turn to **238**.

To research the six companies, turn to **233**.

To visit the compound, turn to **18**.

154

Chtylok pauses its struggles. "Khaw?" it says, and although it's still really loud, it's quieter than it was. She-Hulk and the Thing freeze for a moment. The monster sits down, slowly shaking its head. On the monitors, Arcade is shrieking in impotent rage, but whatever. The heroes jump off Chtylok's shoulders to land back on the arena floor, and they watch in bemusement as the monster lies down, curls up, and starts snoring.

"I can watch this ugly baby sleep it off until Reed gets here," the Thing says. "Go stop that little weasel Arcade."

What is your {WHEELS WITHIN WHEELS} score?

4 or more: turn to **244**.

3 or less: turn to **290**.

155

No, zero is definitely not an odd number. The definition of an even number is that it is a multiple of 2, and $2*0 = 0$. To put it another way, two even numbers and two odd numbers always add to an even number, and one odd and one even number always add to an odd number. $1+0=1$, which is odd; $2+0=2$, which is even. 0 has to be even. Note the ACHIEVEMENT: *It Goes Up To 11*, and also take **-2 CONCENTRATION**.

Three doors become visible in the grey mists. One shows a flower, one a painting, and the third a statue.

To go through the flower door, turn to **255**.

For the painting door, turn to **264**.

For the statue door, turn to **175**.

156

The kitchen is a barren wilderness of marble and chrome, lovely and cold and, if you're any judge, completely untouched. Gleaming pans hang above the six-ring stove. The sink is clean enough to eat soup from, if you wanted an entire vat of soup. This is not a place of cooking. Take **+1 POWER**.

Five strange sodas are in the vast fridge, looking lonely. From the writing on the cans, you assume they're Japanese, but you can't guess at the flavor.

Then you hear a ticking noise, and as you turn, Jen drags you quickly to one side. The stovetop erupts in a blast of flame. Take **+1 {REASONABLE DOUBT}**.

Now make a trap! test. Roll one die and add your **CONCENTRATION**.

One 7 or more: Jen grabs a heavy casserole from a hook and slams it over the stove before the flame can cause any problems.

6 or less: The burst of flame misses you but sets a cabinet alight. Jen swiftly rips it out of the wall and throws it through the door into back yard. Take **+1 {AFLAME}**.

She shakes her head. "Right. Because of course the stove is a flame-thrower. What next?" She looks at you expectantly.

If you'd like to try the lounge, turn to **147**.

If you'd rather head to the dining room, turn to **52**.

157

"Sure," Jen says. "Look, Teena. We can fight, and we'll probably both take some lumps, but there's no need. I'm not here for the Ringmaster or the Circus of Crime, I promise. We just want a document. Ruby doesn't even care about the stuff you've claimed. Keep it. Let us through, and go relax somewhere comfortable. There's no point risking getting hurt."

Teena's eyes narrow as she considers it. Make a logic test. Roll one die, and add your **CONCENTRATION** to it.

One a 7 or more: Teena shrugs. "Fine." She retreats into the kitchens. Take **+1 CONCENTRATION**.

6 or less: Teena just growls, backs up two feet, and begins a lumbering charge, massive ring-laden fists ready to fly. Jen steps forward, one arm out, and catches Teena by the top of the head. The big woman grunts, but she can't even get close enough to punch. She pushes harder, and Jen twists out of the way, using the woman's own weight to send her flying out the door. After twenty feet, Teena slows for a moment, then just keeps right on going, off into the grounds. Jen shrugs.

Now… "According to the floorplan, the kitchens lead on to the parlor and the dining room," Jen says. "Preferences?"

"How about the parlor?" Turn to **292**.

"Let's try the dining room." Turn to **3**.

158

"What do you mean by 'load-bearing' people," you ask.

"The ones who know how it all hangs together. If you just steal code and devices, you're going to have a brutal learning curve trying to understand what you've obtained. It might take years. Developers fill lots of roles, but the ones you want are the ones who understand the whole system well enough to keep everyone else working profitably, guide development in the right directions, and make sure all the bits fit together. Those are the load-bearing ones, because without them, it all falls down. They're valuable, so they're well-treated, and they all get to go show off at big events like the Expo. The VIP list this year is a who's who of important figures from your six companies, with a scattering of privacy wonks thrown in for good measure."

To ask who's behind the Expo, turn to **227**.

To ask what to expect from the show, turn to **266**.

159

You tap at the keypad for a moment, and it beeps. The door slides open. Well done! Take **+1 {PUZZLER}**.

You enter a corridor with polished wooden floors and off-white walls, decorated sparsely with paintings of futuristic cityscapes. It all looks suspiciously normal. There are simple wooden doors at each end of the corridor with nothing much to distinguish them, except that there's a faint draft of fresh air coming from the door to the right.

She-Hulk looks at you expectantly.

"Let's go left." Turn to **127**.

"Let's go right." Turn to **206**.

160

You sweep the goblets to the floor with a dull clatter, and the liquid in them spills onto the stone. A moment later, there's a bleep, and a panel of vine-covered wall slides aside to reveal a white compartment. A moment later, a pair of long, green snakes wriggle out of the space and take to the air, hissing viciously. Take **+1 {WATCHED}**.

"What?" She-Hulk mutters. "Flying pythons appeared once in 1978, damn it. I think I'm actually offended." The snakes flap toward you, and Jen gets ready to grab them.

This is a very easy fight.

Round one: roll two dice and add your **POWER**. If the total is 7 or more – or you have a **[Stained Machete]** – you win the first round.

Round two: roll two dice and add your **POWER**. If the total is 7 or more – or you have some **[Glop]** – you win the second round.

If you somehow manage to lose both rounds, take **-2 CHARM** in pure shame.

With the snakes disposed of, more vine-covered panels

slide away to reveal a pair of doors onwards. They have plaques this time. One says *Temple*, the other says *Pool*.

For the temple, turn to **166**.

For the pool, turn to **62**.

161

You open the door onto the casino. At a glance, it offers a number of all gaming options, from a small bank of slot machines to card tables, roulette, a craps table, and, along the back, a glittering bar.

A scrawny old man with some tufts of grey hair, grey stubble, indifferent eye makeup, and a red-painted nose is in center of the room. He's wearing an orange shirt with a huge neck ruff and black polka dots, along with baggy red pants, and a powder-blue vest – oh, and he's wobbling back and forth on a unicycle.

He looks over at you both with an expression of unholy glee. "Little Jen, back again! Time to play! Oh happy day!" He breaks off into a surprisingly loud cackle that gets steadily higher and more unhinged.

"Ugh," She-Hulk says, disgusted. "Look, I'll put up with a lot of nonsense, I really will, but this is just too pathetic, even for me. I won't do it." It's not clear who she's talking to.

She slams the door shut again, and marches off. Follow her to **259**.

162

"Go for the power core!" you shout.

She-Hulk nods, and leaps at the thing, punching at the glowing core in the center of its chest.

This is a fight!

Round one: roll two dice and add your **POWER** and, if you have any, your {NOBBLED}. If the total is 13 or more, you win the first round.

Round two: roll two dice and add your **POWER** and, if you have any, your {NOBBLED} and your {TROUBLESOME}. If the total is 13 or more, you win the second round.

The fight ends with the robot in a broken heap, its core shattered, but if you lost either round, She-Hulk does get thrown around a bit, so take **-1 CHARM** and **-1 CONCENTRATION**. Either way, note the ACHIEVEMENT: *Terminator Too*.

To examine the broken robot, turn to **221**.

To check out the garden, turn to **250**.

163

The corridor is about eighty yards in length, and ends in another airlock system like the one through which you entered. Jen presses the button, you cycle the antechamber, and go through into a large white room. It reminds you of a warehouse, except that instead of shelving or storage, it holds several huge banks of computer equipment and a selection of other technical devices. At the far end, there's an absolutely gigantic abomination squeezed into an archway that bristles with electronics.

The abomination is fifteen feet tall, a dark grey mass of gelatinous bulges and strands that constantly wobble, shift, and melt into each other. It glares at you out of one huge, bloodshot human-looking eye for a long moment. Then it *shlorps* forward, out of the archway, barreling down on you like a subway train. Take +1 {SHAKEN}.

Jen leaps forward to engage it, fending off sudden pseudopods as it attempts to drag her into its mass to engulf her. This is a nasty fight.

Round one: roll two dice, add your **POWER**, and subtract your {SPACE ALERT} and {WEIRD VIBES}, if any. If the total is 13 or more, you win the first round.

Round one: roll two dice, add your **POWER**, and subtract your {SPACE ALERT} and {WEIRD VIBES}, if any. If the total is 12 or more, you win the second round.

If you won at least one round, turn to **20**.

If you lost both rounds, turn to **219**.

164

The pleasant walkway leads you out of the woods and across a flowery meadow to a large, gleaming metal brick of a building. This, finally, must be the "barn" they talked about.

If there are any windows, they're disguised from the outside. The walls are patterned to look like they've been assembled from sheets of different metals. Perhaps they even have. The walkway leads to a large, heavy-looking door with a row of five of the strangely lumpy security cameras above it.

If you have {TRANSFORMED} of 1, the cameras are motionless. If you do not, the cameras all spring up to track you: take +2 {COOL}.

The two of you do a quick circuit of the building. There are no other doors, still no windows, and no sign of any people. "Something is messing with the people here," She-Hulk says.

Take +1 {REASONABLE DOUBT} and +1 {WHEELS WITHIN WHEELS}.

"We need to help them. So we're going in. I can force this door, or go through a wall. Your pick."

"The door." Turn to **14**.

"The wall." Turn to **253**.

165

The tired woman watches apathetically as Jen heads over to the card reader and breaks it open. As Jen examines the internals, she peels herself off the wall and ambles over. "Here," she says, and unclips her pass. "Have mine. I quit."

Jen smiles at her gratefully. "Thank you. Are you sure?"

"Just be careful, okay? Something's wrong in there." She studies She-Hulk more carefully. "You already know that. This is *definitely* the best decision I ever made. I just developed an urgent appointment with Redondo Beach."

"That sounds like a great move. Thanks again."

The woman smiles at her, her face lighting up. "Good luck, hero." She departs at a pace just one notch below a flat-out run.

Jen swipes the card, and it opens. You walk through into a small stretch of beige corridor. There are three frosted glass doors at the other end, one directly ahead and the other two set in the walls opposite each other. One is red, one is green, the last is blue.

"I've got a bad feeling about this," Jen says. "Which door would you pick?"

"Red." Turn to **194**.

"Green." Turn to **178**.

"Blue." Turn to **298**.

166

The temple is a large space designed in the ancient Greek style, with two rows of fluted marble columns bordering the room. The floor is also marble, polished to a shine, and there's a large, blocky altar at the far end. You guessed it, it's made of marble too. The towering statue behind the altar is not marble, however. It's an orange color, apart from the blue of its apparent trunks, and in terms of bulk, it looks a bit like a smooth version of the Thing. The most disturbing thing about it is the way that its unknown sculptor elongated its head, and gave it two snarling faces stacked on top of each other.

Beside you, She-Hulk tenses. "The Bi-Beast," she mutters. "That's really not ideal."

The statue growls, its expression darkening further, and steps over the altar, heading for you!

How well-warned are your enemies at this point? If your {WATCHED} is 1 to 3, set your {PENALTY} to 1. If it is 4 to 6, set {PENALTY} to 2. If it's 7 or more, set {PENALTY} to 3.

"We know you," the monster says from its lower face, its voice like crushed rock. "You are like Hulk, but smaller."

"Weaker," adds the upper face.

Jen scowls. "Now that's just *rude*. You're not even the original. How many times have you been defeated, anyway? I lose track. Is it … 5?"

As the beast lumbers toward you, Jen fills you in quickly, "Bi-Beast is an alien android. It doesn't feel pain or fatigue, and it's horribly strong. It's clever, but not really up on Earth tech. Any suggestions?"

"Try damaging it?" Turn to **78**.

"Try outmaneuvering it?" Turn to **87**.

"Try bluffing?" Turn to **144**.

167

You tuck in against the wall of the main building. You can hear drones somewhere nearby, but they are not in sight right at the moment. She-Hulk turns to look at the wall suspiciously, and raps a knuckle on it. It thuds hollowly. "I don't want to tear this open unless there's no choice, but there's a door hidden here. Got anything sharp that you don't really need?"

Do you have a [Sword] you're happy to contribute to the cause? If so, you hand it over, and she uses it to lever the door open. Remove it from your inventory and turn to **300**.

Otherwise, the pair of you have to move on, edging around the side of the building. Turn to **71**.

168

She-Hulk rolls Kangaroo around slightly so that he's looking upwards, and then stands over him. "Who hired you, Brian?"

Kangaroo sighs bitterly. "Strewth, Red. I don't know, and that's dead set. Played me for a right galah. Did it all over the lappy, through me mate. Paid me in those bite coins, and some sort of fancy link to a little picture of a monkey. Come here, grab the Sheila, guard the old buzzard upstairs, then let her loose, and rack off again on Sunday night. Supposed to be gnarly, no worries. Then you show up, and now I'm headed back inside. I'm devo, I tell ya."

She pats him on the cheek. "It could be much worse, I promise. You've still got all your limbs, and that's not nothing. Now lie here like a good boy until the police collect you."

To head up into the hotel, turn to **31**.

To take a moment to recover first, turn to **124**.

169

"Firm," you mutter. Jen nods. She strides across the room, as implacable as the sunrise, until she's standing right up against the desk and looking the judge firmly in the eye.

"You know who I am and why I'm here," Jen says, her voice flat. "So you know that Ms Rubinstein's arrest is at the very best completely irregular, and that it was something that you should never have been involved with in any way. You almost certainly know my reputation well enough to be aware that your only remaining choice at this point is whether you take this one chance I'm offering, or I leave your career ground into dust."

Take +1 {WAVES} and +1 {SMARTS}.

The woman goes an unhealthy shade of grey, and wobbles on her feet. "I..." she manages.

Jen's tone lightens into sympathy. "Who do they have – and do you really believe they'll let them go? The body count on this hideous nightmare is *already* in triple digits. I'm your only chance."

The judge collapses into her chair. "My sister. They have my sister. Marion. They said... Get her back, I beg you."

"Who?"

"I don't know. They took her outside a bar. She was going to meet an ex. He might know something. I also asked some quiet questions, and there's a CI who's often round that area. He's another possibility. I didn't dare risk it, but..." She swallows. "Triple digits? Dear God."

Jen spends some time comforting the judge, and assuring her that everything will be fine.

To try to find the ex, turn to **5**.

To find the informant, turn to **212**.

170

The badge door leads into a psychedelic cardboard city. Buildings of all sorts surround you, two dimensional and far too bright. You watch, bemused, as a cut-out of a dayglo green taxi cab trundles past.

Suddenly a burst of gunfire shreds the taxi. Jen steps forward and, past her, you see a clanking robot wearing a police uniform and carrying a boxy alien gun-like device. Another one rolls up behind it, and then another. "Stay down," Jen says urgently, and leaps toward them.

Make a force test. Roll two dice and add your **POWER** and **CONCENTRATION**. If you have **[Spiked Knuckles]**, add **+3**. If the total is 12 or less, take **-2 POWER** from the hail of bullets as She-Hulk closes on the robots.

She grabs one robot and uses it to smash the other two into scrap, and then clears the cardboard scenery with it. There are two doors onwards, one marked with a square, the other with a circle.

For the square door, turn to **247**.

For the circle door, turn to **215**.

171

You loiter by the coffee concession for a few minutes, until you see a likely target – a black-suited man absorbed in a sheaf of printouts is heading straight for the restricted section. You fall in behind him, and hurry through smartly as he does so.

The doors are closing behind you when he stops, then turns and looks at the pair of you. "I'd know if I'd seen a green woman before," he says. He sounds a little surprised.

"We work with Neil Gould," Jen says blandly.

"Oh," the man says. "Gould." He clearly doesn't like him very much. He shrugs and bustles off, but he shoots a suspicious glance in your direction as he does so.

Is he concerned? Make an innocence test. Roll one die and add your **CHARM**.

Roll a 7 or more: turn to **117**.

6 or less: turn to **232**.

172

"What does 'total information control' actually mean in practice?" you ask.

"Power on a level that most dictators can only dream of," Ruby says. "At the very least, hijack any information being transmitted anywhere on the Internet and copy, stop, or even alter it in real time. Depending on how good AnxiousChimp's systems are, probably infiltrate any system that you can find an access point for. Banking, air traffic control, police, military systems. We've outsourced all of society's maintenance functions to computers. Theoretically, this is limitless."

"Why AnxiousChimp?" Jen asks.

"You have to understand that all six of the targeted companies are multi-headed. We all do a lot of things. But we're all developing some systems that are far beyond the cutting edge, and those are the pillars that make this total control system such a powerful proposition. In the case of AnxiousChimp, it's a qBit device for decrypting arbitrarily large hashes, funded by the military. An encryption-buster, simply. Hack anything.

"Meanwhile, I'm developing a hyper-flexible networking substrate to connect any system to any other. The other pieces are data extraction and filtration, self-training information tagging and cross-referencing, cognitive modeling, and the pattern recognition system you found at Tekeli that will let the platform convert what it's seeing into usable data, strip the signal out of the noise. It's a real witches' brew."

"But surely–" you begin.

"The first thing you do with this system is suppress any reference to yourself, your location, the stolen code, and any other weak points. Suddenly, no law enforcement agent – or super hero, for that matter – can even hear about or refer to you unless it's in person or hard-copy. Phone calls just drop. Emails never arrive. Database searches come up blank. It would take days to even begin to cobble together a response, and by then, you control it all."

Jen looks absolutely horrified, and you're sure you must as well. You suddenly feel cold and clammy.

"Ah," Ruby says, satisfied. "Now you get it."

ACHIEVEMENT: *The End of the World Again.*

"I like that story," Jen says. "It's a nice homage."

To ask what Ruby meant about "load-bearing" people, turn to **158**.

To ask what to expect from the Expo, turn to **266**.

173

She-Hulk blinks, then punches Bessie in the chest. The vampire cow is flung back twenty feet, but quickly slows to a hover, and laughs her awful, mooing laugh. She floats down to the ground, still standing upright on her back hooves, and bares her fangs to hiss horribly. You note with curiosity that she still has her original teeth in addition to her curved, gleaming fangs, but her tongue is much longer and thinner than it should be. You're going to have to have words with your subconscious when you wake up.

Another flicker, and Bessie is back in front of She-Hulk again, lashing out with a savagely fast razor hoof to the face. Somehow, the blow doesn't quite land, sliding through the empty space where Jen's head had surely just been. They exchange a flurry of blows, attacks and blocks and counterpunches. Then there's a fluid, twisting disturbance you can't follow, and Bessie is smashed down onto her back. She immediately rolls sideways, avoiding a savage stomp, and springs to her feet – uh, her back hooves – before advancing again.

This is a fight!

Round one: roll two dice and add your **POWER**. If the total is 7 or more, you win the first round.

Round two: roll two dice and add your **POWER**. If you won the first round, add 1. If your total is 8 or more, you win the second round.

If you won the second round, turn to **201**.

If you lost the second round, turn to **38**.

174

Bi-Beast looks at you both for a long time. "We think you are lying," it eventually says.

"Are you willing to gamble your existence on that, for a cause that does not matter to you?"

"We have been promised much."

"You believed that idiot?" Jen counters. "You know how deceitful humans are." It doesn't immediately reply. "Weigh your options. Leave this place, harming none, and continue your existence. Remain and be obliterated in service to a false promise given by a liar."

You can hear its teeth grind. Then, amazingly, its palms begin glowing, and it lifts into the air. It crunches straight through the ceiling and two more levels of the complex, and is gone.

Jen sighs in relief. "Renee would never have let Byrne put me through that. Hey, I wonder if that was Ben's scary signal. I don't think Bi-Beast is quite enough to panic Reed Richards, but hey, who knows. Either way, it's gone. Good work with the menacing doodad."

Take +1 **POWER** and the ACHIEVEMENT: *Menacing Doodads*.

Past the altar, you spy a couple of doors. One is stenciled with a coffee cup icon, the other with a washbasin.

"What do you think?" She-Hulk asks.

"I could use a coffee." Turn to **299**.

"How about the washroom?" Turn to **26**.

175

The statue door leads into a sparse room with a thick, red-orange carpet and terracotta-colored walls. No other doors are obviously visible. Three stone statues stand in the middle of the room, each one an identical impression of a person – the right shape, with arms and legs, but no features. Each statue is holding an identical red velvet pouch.

As you examine this odd set-up, a clearly computerized voice speaks from below the center statue. "Each bag holds two similar balls. In one, both are white. In another, both are black. In the third, there is one of each. If you take one ball out of one bag at random, and discover it is white, what is the chance that the other ball in that bag is also white? You may speak your answer."

What do you say?

"Two thirds." Turn to **11**.

"One half." Turn to **105**.

176

The information booth is tucked under a staircase at the end of a hallway that leads from the game hall to the restrooms. The glass outer wall is jammed with attractive cosplayers selling photo opportunities, all of them thronged. Progress is at a snail's pace at best. When you eventually get to the booth, you discover that the line stretches back almost to the other end of the hallway.

You wait and wait, inching forward. Everyone seems to assume Jen is a cosplayer. Mostly, you're left alone, apart from one smug man who spends half a minute informing Jen that she's too short to pull off a good She-Hulk. Amazingly, she doesn't beat him to a pulp.

Eventually the unhappy looking person behind the desk gestures for you to come forward.

"Where's the VIP area?" Jen asks.

The person actually groans and rolls their eyes.

"*Please*," Jen adds, as nicely as she can manage.

Make a persuasion test. Roll one die and add your **CHARM**. If the total is 12 or more, or if you have {EXPO PASS} of 1, you are directed sullenly but far faster, to **75**.

Otherwise, the person says, "That's in the VIP welcome

packet. Which you don't have. Because you're not a VIP." They're already calling the next attendee up. Take **-1 CONCENTRATION** in frustration damage.

To try the games hall, turn to **263**.

To try the food court, turn to **54**.

To wander the complex hoping to spot something, turn to **88**.

177

Ringmaster has prepared well, it turns out. As She-Hulk leaps, he activates a device across the room that emits blinding flashes of light in waves. You can't see a thing. When Jen smashes it and you regain your sight, Ringmaster and his companion are gone. It takes a couple of minutes to find the hidden exit they used, inside a false cabinet, by which time there's no point following.

It only takes a moment more to open Ruby's files and download the video recording which definitively shows her here, in this room, on a call with a bunch of independent witnesses at the time of Bright's death. She-Hulk copies it onto two separate USB drives for safety. Then she calls the police, warning them that the mansion is only partly secured and there might still be a bunch of showy but indifferently-aggressive thugs on the loose.

What do you suggest doing while you wait for them?

Research Ruby's case? Turn to **133**.

Call up Ruby and update her? Turn to **281**.

178

You pass through the green door into a space filled with dense fog. There's some ambient yellow light coming from somewhere, but you can't pinpoint the source. The floor feels sticky, and you can make out that you're sloshing through some sort of glop.

A wave of fatigue washes through you, making your feet prickle. Your feet? "I... think we're walking in something toxic," you realize at last.

Are you in time? Make an awareness test. Roll one die and add your Concentration. If the total is 9 or less, take **-1 POWER** and **-1 CONCENTRATION**.

She-Hulk sweeps you up off the floor and carries you. She ignores the glop. You find two doors hidden in the fog, one bearing a mailbox icon and the other a cop's shield – but before you go, you may collect some **[Glop]** in an empty water bottle.

To try the mailbox door, turn to **33**.

To try the badge door, turn to **170**.

179

Spellcheck shrieks, dashes to a wall, fumbles for a moment, then drops into a trapdoor. While the pair of you stare, you hear him outside, still shrieking as he flees.

"Wow," She-Hulk says. "Just wow. They really do give me all the *best* villains."

Take **+1 {REASONABLE DOUBT}**.

The pair of you look around the attic. At the back of the space, you find a huge corkboard pinned with maps, photographs, scraps of newspaper article, and a dazzling web of red thread connecting it all. A large Thurstech logo is pinned near the heart of the chaos. You start carefully photographing everything. Take +1 {MURDERBOARD}.

"Do you think we have enough to go on, or would you rather search Bright's workplace?" She-Hulk asks you.

"We've got enough." Turn to **252**.

"Better safe than sorry." Turn to **191**.

180

Bi-Beast smashes She-Hulk to the floor, and you hear her groan in pain. It lifts a foot to stamp down on her, but Jen seizes its ankle and heaves. The monster collapses back onto the ground with a crash that makes the floor shake. As it gets up again, Jen retreats back toward the altar, luring it away from you.

This is a very hard fight.

Round one: roll two dice, add your **POWER**, and subtract your {PENALTY}. If the total is 13 or more, you win the first round.

Round two: roll two dice, add your **POWER**, and subtract

your {PENALTY}. If the total is 14 or more, you win the second round.

Round three: roll two dice, add your POWER, and subtract your {PENALTY}. If the total is 13 or more, you win the third round.

If you won at least two rounds, turn to **256**.

If you lost at least two rounds, however, turn to **228**.

181

It's difficult to follow the fight, but She-Hulk forces Bessie back repeatedly, staying close to the tree. Finally she grabs the vampire by the throat. Bessie explodes into mist again for a moment, but as she reforms she's already hovering. She hisses once, a long, low sound full of irritation and spite, and then retreats up into the air, fading slowly into the night sky as she flees.

She-Hulk looks at the metal bell she ripped from around the cow's neck. "Souvenir?" You may add the [Evil Cowbell] to your inventory.

"Is she gone?" you ask.

"Yes. She can't beat me, and now she's sure of it. She didn't survive four centuries of bovine undeath without knowing when to retreat."

Add the ACHIEVEMENT: *Mooooo*. (The complete set of collectible achievements are listed at the back of the book. Go check it off or, if this is an ebook, make a note of it somewhere handy. OK, or there, if you must.)

"I guess this is where I wake up, then?"

She smiles sympathetically. "I completely understand your doubt, but you really are awake – this is the real world. Bessie genuinely is an ancient vampire cow, and she did just attack us." She pauses for a moment. "OK, it's been a weird day."

"Right," you say hesitantly. "Weird. Sure."

"Look, the quick version is I'm considering a new client. I don't have offices in California, so I need local help. You. But I'm also between permanent paralegals, so you can consider this an extended interview. That's why I asked for your input on how to approach Bessie. Whether you know it or not, you've got someone extremely special looking over your shoulder. I'll do my very best to keep you safe – and my best is very good indeed. We can make a real difference together. Are you in?"

You nod. If you are really awake, this just became the best day ever. "Yes, Mi— Jen. All in. Weirdness or not."

She smiles. "Great! I think we've got a few moments. Do you want the background on the client now?"

"Yes, please." Turn to **192**.

"May I catch up later?" Turn to **211**.

182

In short order, Judge Hirst is reunited with her sister and Jen is handed immediate release papers for Ruby. The judge's delight is tempered with fear, but that vanishes when Jen reassures her that as far as she's concerned, the bail refusal was an unfortunate misunderstanding which they resolved amicably.

"I can't thank you enough," the judge says. "The last few days have been utter hell. Any moment, I was expecting one or more hammers to fall and crush me."

Jen smiles. "Thank you for trusting me to help."

"Speaking of which, if I can ever repay the favor, just say so." Take **+1 {LEGAL FAVOR}**.

"I'll remember that," Jen promises sincerely. "Thank you."

You take Ruby's bail papers back to the jail, and in about ten minutes, she is released to join you. She's projecting the same red-haired head as she used in the prison, and wearing a very sharp, well-tailored pant suit, charcoal with crimson lining, along with a matching crimson blouse.

As she approaches, she breaks into a genuine-looking smile that takes in both of you. "Good to see you again," she says. "I would normally insert some pleasantries and small talk, but time is of the essence." Jen nods. "If we're going to work out what this is all about, I need to know what Shine Today and Tekeli Industries are really up to. Tekeli are a little wary of me, so I'll leave them to you and take Shine. I don't recommend trying to sneak onto the Tekeli premises, but my contact there is an executive named Neil Gould. He's got a fondness for a very expensive Turkish delicacy that I keep him supplied with. So I can either call my supplier and arrange for you take in a delivery, or I can call Neil and set up an actual appointment with you as supposed employees, but you'll have to attend that. Your call."

She-Hulk looks at you.

To suggest the delivery option, turn to **92**.

To suggest the meeting, turn to **113**.

183

The lectern door leads you through a curtain onto a modest stage. There's a desk on the stage, and sharply-rising rows of seats looking down on you. Happily, the seats are empty. The desk holds a sheet of paper, and it's covered in numbers and letters.

This is a puzzle!

A	A	B	A	103
A	B	B	C	103
B	A	C	A	96
B	C	B	C	206
110	96	110	?	

To progress, turn to the entry equal to the value of that last "?" entry. If the first words you see there are not "You solved the lectern!", you can return here and try again.

Alternatively, retreat to the room with the badge door by turning to **170**.

184

The laboratory is enigmatic, to say the least. Some of it is perfectly ordinary – the computer workstations, the chalkboard with a double-underlined "*Pivot to Rb*" scrawled across it, the aspidistra plant. There are various familiar-looking devices and bits of equipment you don't necessarily remember the names for, but at least you've seen them before.

Then there's the other stuff, which is not so ordinary. A shiny metal globe, about a foot across, with a dozen regularly-spaced circular indentations which hangs in the air over a bench. Something that looks like a hand-scanner designed for a hand with far too many fingers, very thin ones at that. A network of crystal nodes spread right across one wall, connected with filaments that phase in and out of visibility, with glowing points of light navigating along them at about walking speed. Meanwhile, out of sight, some device or other is emitting a sound that's almost too low to hear, but it makes your innards itch unpleasantly. The two of you stare for a long moment.

"Huh," Jen says eventually, shaking her large head.

Across the lab, there's a door that looks exactly like an airlock out of any sci-fi movie of your choice – lots of thick metal, red warning lights, a small glass porthole, threateningly large buttons, the works.

To check out the airlock, turn to **107**.

To poke at the weird gadgets, turn to **199**.

To head back across the corridor to the glowing room, turn to **276**.

185

The late Anthony Bright lived in a decidedly upscale area. The houses are very large and attractively designed, set in generous lots that skew heavy on leafy trees, well-trimmed hedgerows, and ornamental lawns. Even the sidewalks are tree-lined. The water bills must be astronomical.

Bright's house looks like a generous family home from a Norman Rockwell painting, except that he didn't put in a white picket fence. According to the notes, he lived there alone, not uncommon for a high-flying wonder-nerd in his twenties. It could be a show-home – there's nothing personal about the place, not from the outside at least. Like buying this multi-million-dollar house was something he'd ticked off a list, and then mostly forgotten about. Nice work if you can get it.

A young woman walking a shaggy dog strolls past, gawping at the pair of you, but at least she doesn't tut.

"We don't have keys," Jen says. "Would you go in through the front or the back?"

"The front." Turn to **236**.

"The back." Turn to **44**.

186

Oort is flung back several feet. He's doubled over and trying to catch his breath, watching Jen warily as Ruby closes on him from the side. She's stopped blasting Big Wheel, but he's still spinning so fast that the wheel looks more like a sphere. Once she's less than ten feet away, several of the tentacles projecting from her head dart down and grab Oort, lifting him into the air. He struggles, turning to face her, plasma welling up in his gloved hand.

She-Hulk steps up and punches him so hard that he's flung out of Ruby's grasp and into the whirling chaos that is Big Wheel. There's a horrible crash, and the wheel goes careening off to smash into the wall of the restaurant area in a shower of sparks and debris. The whine of its engine vanishes. Oort staggers to his feet, looking dazed. Jen and Ruby immediately leap on him.

This is an easy mop-up. Roll two dice and add your **POWER** and **CHARM** to factor in Ruby's help.

Score a 9 or more: Turn to **40**.

8 or less: Turn to **295**.

187

Jen nods approvingly. "Good move. You can't dodge in mid-air. Less chance of unintentional injury." Take **+1 CONCENTRATION**.

She advances on the bouncing twins, and as she gets close to them, she snatches up a table like a very oversized shield. There's a pair of solid impacts, and then the acrobats are on the floor, groaning. She looks down at them sternly. "Do I have to tie you up?"

They look at each other sheepishly. "No, Miss," one says. He has a strong European accent. He crosses himself. "I swear it. We leave you alone."

"And no harming the mansion," she says.

"No, Miss," says the other one.

She nods brusquely. "Good." She leaves them rubbing sore heads, and returns to you. "From here, we can try the library or the cloakroom."

"The library." Turn to **64**.

"The cloakroom." Turn to **291**.

188

Jen dials the jail and you wait a while. After a minute or two, Ruby's voice comes over the speaker. "Hi, Jen."

"Hello, Ruby. Good news. The judge who refused your bail was being blackmailed. We have resolved that threat, and are about to head over to give her the good news. You should be out shortly."

"Excellent work. You'll meet me at the gates here?"

"Of course."

"I'll see you soon then." She hangs up. Take **+1 {SYMPATICO}**.

To get Marion back to the judge, turn to **182**.

To interview her first, turn to **118**.

189

"Now, now, my dear. That was rude. But no matter, we'll adjust that fiery temper of yours, and oh, I'm sorry to tell you that I don't need you to look at either my hat or myself."

An instant later, She-Hulk groans.

Do you have the [Slim File]? If so, you've flicked through it enough to know that Ruby's secure office has excellent fire protection. You know where the trigger button is for powder extinguisher, so you dash over and press it. Thick clouds of sweet-smelling powder fill the room. Turn to **231**.

If you're still here, you'll have to do this the old-fashioned way. Make a willpower test. Roll one die, add your **CONCENTRATION** and your **POWER**, and subtract your {INTENSITY}, if any.

Get an 11 or more: Turn to **231**.

10 or less: Turn to **77**.

190

You've found a secret entry. Well done! The suspicious broccoli icon points roughly to a pictogram of a snarling wolf, and when you firmly trace your finger over the route between the two, a light embedded in the control panel springs into life for a moment.

There's a flash of blue-white light from behind you, so bright that it leaves sunspots on your vision for several seconds. You turn around nervously, but the big glass panel is still a dark abyss. However, on the floor in front of it is a shiny metal glove. It would fit She-Hulk, and it crackles with potential. You may take it if you like and you have room – the [Experimental Gauntlet] increases your **POWER** by 2 as long as it is in your inventory. ACHIEVEMENT: *Secret Two.*

To study the glass panel, turn to **225**.

To leave the room, turn to **206**.

191

Bright worked for a company called Omni and Grey. They have several sites, but the one you need is up in the hills. The company's website refers to it affectionately as "The Barn."

After a long drive out into the middle of nowhere, the road ends in a tall, barred gate. There's a security hut there, and as you pull up, a guard comes out to meet you. She-Hulk rolls the window down.

"This is Omni and Grey. Can we help you?" he asks pleasantly.

Make an observation test. Roll one die, and add your **CONCENTRATION** to it. If the total is 7 or more, you spot an unusually large security camera swivel to focus on you. Take **+1 {COOL}**.

"Jennifer Walters, attorney-at-law. I'd like to speak to someone about Anthony Bright."

The man smiles. If he's in the least bit surprised by the sudden appearance of Herculean green lawyer, he's hiding it very well. Then again, this is the hills outside Silicon

Valley. He probably spends his lunch break with a bigfoot family. "Of course. We are one. Please wait a moment." The guard vanishes into his hut for a minute or so.

Corporations have catchphrases now? Weird. You share a look with Jen. She obviously thinks he's as odd as you do.

He returns after a few moments. "Please go on through to the visitor's lodge. Ken Winton will meet you there."

The gate slides back, and you drive into the woodland that the complex is in. After a few hundred yards, you see the lodge – and a big staff café – near a small visitor's car-park.

"Are we feeling obedient today?" She-Hulk asks.

To go to the lodge as directed, turn to **152**.

To head to the café instead, turn to **74**.

192

As you start walking again, Jen explains. "I'm investigating an old enemy of mine, a villain named Thursday Rubinstein, Ruby. She's CEO of a Silicon Valley company called Thurstech now, a wildly successful one. That's no surprise – she's a genuine super-genius, one of the most intelligent people on the entire planet, and she has a real special talent for computing, electronics, and engineering. Two days ago, she was arrested for the murder of a top programmer working at a competitor's company, a guy named Anthony Bright."

You nod. So far, reasonably straightforward.

"The cops say her prints are all over his life, both literally and metaphorically, and the weapon that killed him is hers. There are no other suspects. Her side of it is that they were in advanced discussions to have him come work for her, she's never owned a firearm of any type, and she's being framed, because… well, actually, she has no idea. She claims to be wealthier and more powerful as a tech entrepreneur than she ever was as a villain, as well as a lot safer day to day, and that it would be ludicrous to imagine she'd jeopardize that by backsliding. She always was the calculating type, so that's certainly plausible."

"Okay."

"Obviously, if she *has* given up crime, I want to support her all the way. She's incredibly dangerous as a criminal. But she's tried to take me out before, so blind trust is off the table. That's why she wants me as her lawyer. She knows our personal history will play well to the jury, since I have every reason to dislike and distrust her. It's a clever move, as you'd expect. So that's why we're here. Bright was killed around here, not far from that ornamental fountain. I'm hoping we can find some trace evidence either way."

It's a little more tangled than most cases, but it makes sense. "Got it," you say.

She-Hulk hesitates, then presses on. "I should probably also tell you that Ruby doesn't have a head."

"Wait. What?"

"Blame *Defenders* #32. Her head was replaced years ago with a big shining red orb of organic circuitry. I don't know how. It's where her intellect comes from. She can make it look like a real head, sprout long tentacles from it, fire energy beams from it, separate it from her body while keeping control of both, and even make it temporarily explode with enough power to knock the Hulk out."

Okay, *there's* the crazy you were expecting. You latch onto one of the last things you heard. "*Temporarily explode?*"

She sighs. "It reforms."

"Is it always like this?"

She pauses. "Yeah."

"Thanks for telling me." You think it over for a moment. "I'm still in."

"Excellent answer. So, what do you make of Bessie's presence?"

"If I'd killed someone and wanted it to look low-profile, I certainly wouldn't set a vampire cow to watch over the murder site. But if I was framing a super-villain, I might well want to drive off anyone who came digging."

Jen nods approvingly. "Exactly what I was thinking."

Take +1 {REASONABLE DOUBT}. Secondary stats are always in {CURLY BRACKETS}, and start at 0. Since this is the first time you've come across it, your {REASONABLE DOUBT} is now 1. Keep track of them as they change how events unfold.

"So, where would you start looking?" she asks.

To check out the murder site, turn to **282**.

To start with the thicket of trees, turn to **237**.

To examine the area near the fountain, turn to **94**.

Jen nods, and pushes the door open with no more sign of effort than when she'd tried it a moment ago. There's a sharp crack, and the door opens easily. Take **+1 POWER**.

Inside, you see a generous hallway tiled in soft terracotta tones. Past the bare vestibule just inside the door, there are a couple of doorways leading deeper into the house.

Oh, and there's also a weird-looking shotgun-like device on a stand pointing straight at you, its trigger wired to the door you just opened.

Click.

Take **+1 {REASONABLE DOUBT}**. Now make a trap! test. Roll one die, and add your **POWER**.

Total of 6 or more: Jen has already blurred into the hallway, and she grabs the device as it goes off. It discharges harmlessly into the ceiling.

5 or less: The device goes off, blasting her full in the torso. She's completely unharmed, but it does rip a nasty hole in her nicely tailored suit. She sighs. "That's... annoying." Take **-1 CHARM**. "Come on in, and keep an eye open for other traps."

Through the doorways ahead, you can see what looks like a lounge to the left, and maybe a home office to the right.

To head left, turn to **147**.

To go right, turn to **25**.

194

You pass through the red door... and onto an alien planet. Space looms around and above you, dotted with impossibly distant stars. The ground is grey and particulate, like crushed volcanic pumice, and stretches off into the distance. Weak red light comes from the undersides of tall, fungus-like structures that appear to be dripping with gore.

You're standing there frozen when She-Hulk says, "My weight hasn't changed."

"Eh?" you manage.

She turns and punches at the air behind her. There's a loud crack, and the screen cobwebs. A moment later, the display walls all crash to white. Huh.

The room's not actually that big. A couple of doors lead onwards, one stenciled with a scroll icon, the other with a mailbox. The one actual goreshroom cracks open to reveal... a vending machine?

What?

Peering in, you see that the machine offers three ugly items – [Spiked Knuckles], a [Stained Machete], or a [Claw Glove]. If you have a [Fungal Token], you may swap it for one of the three.

"Why would that work in here?" Jen mutters. "Oddly convenient, don't you think?"

Which door do you recommend now?

For the scroll door, turn to **63**.

For the mailbox door, turn to **33**.

195

You got the puzzle wrong, and the keypad has locked you out. On the plus side, you do get a nice reward for being honest about it! Take **+2 {CHARM}**and the ACHIEVEMENT: *Virtue is its Own Reward*.

You need to try another route through the mansion. Pick an entry point below that you haven't already tried yet.

The kitchens: turn to **10**.

The pool: turn to **272**.

The guest suite: turn to **43**.

196

She-Hulk just stands there as the man points his little laser pistol at her and opens fire. You drop to the floor and clamp your hands over your ears as loud zapping noises fill the room. There's a sudden, loud metallic clank that sounds painful even over the laser, and then everything goes quiet.

You get up to find She-Hulk standing over the big, now unconscious man, going through his wallet. "He calls himself Cool Million. Huh. He looks more like a Barry to me." She tosses the wallet back onto his chest.

ACHIEVEMENT: *Not So Cool Now, Huh?*

By the time the pair of you have him securely trussed, blindfolded and gagged, the Omni and Grey people are starting to wake up. They seem perfectly normal now, if somewhat traumatized by what they've been through. They happily give you Anthony Bright's files – the ones that aren't commercially sensitive anyway – and call for the authorities to send someone to take care of the psychotic hypno-mutant. One of the files contains a weird [Fungal Token] that you can take if you like.

If any of your POWER, CHARM, or CONCENTRATION are below 2, set them to 2 now, and set {FILES} to 1. If you still have a mug of [Coffee] with you, you may drink it for a further +1 CONCENTRATION.

If you want to search Bright's home and haven't done so, turn to **185**.

If you want to start putting your evidence together, turn to **252**.

197

You walk down a short but weirdly tall tunnel, then out into a brightly lit arena clearly inspired by movies about gladiators. It's oval, with a sandy floor and surrounding walls ten feet high. Tiered rows of stone benches surround the space, rising up toward the ceiling – at least fifty feet high. At the center of one long edge, where you'd expect to see Caesar's imperial box, there's a large cluster of video screens.

As you stand there taking it all in, the screens flicker to life. They're all displaying the same image of a slender man in his thirties, with a shock of floppy red hair. He's wearing a white three-piece suit paired with an eye-searingly green shirt and an equally garish purple bow tie, and he's lounging back in a big leather executive chair. He has the biggest, smuggest grin you've ever seen. The screens flicker, then display the image as a composite spread across all of them. You can't help wincing. A man whose colors clash that badly has no business looking smug.

"She-Hulk," he purrs. "You *came*. And you even kept your trusty assistant alive through my Murderworld. I'm glad."

Jen stares for a long moment. "Arcade," she says, her voice full of disbelief, and promptly dissolves into uncontrollable sniggering.

Arcade scowls bitterly.

"I'm sorry," Jen manages, in between howls of amusement. "I just–". She breaks off, gets herself under control, and wipes away a tear. "I was expecting someone… taller."

How's your mental resilience? If your {SHAKEN} is 1 to 3, set your {WOBBLY} to 1. If it is 4 to 6, set {WOBBLY} to 2. If it's 7 or more, set {WOBBLY} to 3.

Arcade plasters that obnoxious grin back on his face, but his eyes look furious. "Let me help you with that."

A very high-pitched note sounds across the arena, and an absolutely colossal figure lumbers onto the sand at the far end. It's vast, at least twenty-five feet tall, with bright red eyes and a wicked looking beak. Despite the bird head, the top half of its body looks like someone gave King Kong a thick coating of white feathers, and its brown tree-trunk legs appear to have come from the largest minotaur in existence. It fixes you with its beady red eyes. "*Kraw!!*" it bellows, the sound deafening even from sixty feet away.

"Oh brother," Jen says. She quickly pulls out her phone and tosses it to you. "Call Ben. We found his anomaly." You catch the phone and start texting.

"Tall enough for you?" Arcade gloats. "Allow me to introduce–"

"Chtylok," Jen cuts in. "The Chicken Cow. I know."

"The Che-K'n Kau," Arcade says fussily. Is he pouting?

"That's what I said."

Arcade pinches the bridge of his nose. "Chtylok, *kill!*"

"*Kraw!*" The beast springs, hurtling through the air toward you. She-Hulk leaps into the air to intercept it.

Make a mid-air tussle test. Roll one die, add your **CONCENTRATION** and **POWER**, then subtract your {WOBBLY}.

Score 14 or more: turn to **146**.

13 or less: turn to **6**.

198

"We've got to go in there," Jen says. "The VIPs don't realize that they're on a hit list, and we've got to keep them out of the clutches of the maniac pulling the strings. If your big scary signal is part of this, I'll find it."

"You be careful," the Thing says seriously. "I mean it."

"Of course."

"You're still on the cell that ends ... 26, right?"

The two of them compare numbers.

Ben sighs. "I'm dancing to Reed's tune for now, but if you find that thing, you call and wait for me get there. Whatever it is, it's nasty. If I find out anything, I'll let you know."

"It's a deal," Jen promises.

To ask whether he knows where the VIP area is, turn to **34**.

To ask if he's seen anything suspicious, turn to **270**.

199

The strange lab equipment is just too fascinating to ignore. You're drawn to it like a moth to a flame. The globe really is floating. There's nothing above or below it. You poke it with a handy pencil, but it just wobbles a little before returning to its previous position. It seems a little heavier than you would think, given how much effort it takes to move it, but only a little.

The strange sound is not exactly louder over here, but it's more intense. It might be fluctuating slightly with the progress of the light orbs across the crystal lattice, but it's hard to tell. You get the impression that you're only hearing the tiniest fraction of the sound, and you still can't place its source.

Then the globe spins rapidly, stopping with one indentation directly aimed at your head. The indentation fills with light. Make a luck test: Roll one die, and subtract your {SPACE ALERT}, if any.

Score 4-6: The light wells out, settling around you for a moment. Take +1 {ILLUMINATED}.

1-3: The light zaps out in a beam, striking you in the forehead. Take +1 {LIT UP}.

Note the ACHIEVEMENT: *The Experimentalist.*

You stagger back from the globe on reflex, but nothing seems to immediately happen. Probably a close escape. Discretion is almost certainly the better part of valor when messing with what looks like alien tech.

She-Hulk arches an eyebrow at you, and you shrug, a little shame-faced. What now?

To check out the airlock, turn to **107**.

To head back across the corridor to the glowing room, turn to **276**.

200

There's a brief flurry of action, tough to follow in the dim attic, then She-Hulk has Spellcheck in a firm armlock. ACHIEVEMENT: *Clippy.*

"Wow, thanks for reminding me of *that* thing. Meanie." She shakes her head. "What were they thinking? And you. Will you stop this nonsense now?" she asks.

"Yes, Miss," Spellcheck says.

She rolls her eyes. "Why are you in this house?"

"I was hired to guard it from snoopers," he says.

"By who?"

"It was all over the Darkweb."

She frowns at him. "That wasn't the question."

"Okay! Don't hurt me!"

"I haven't," She-Hulk says with exaggerated patience.

"Well, don't!"

"Who hired you?"

"Their username was RThurStein," Spellcheck says sullenly.

"Of course it was."

Make an adrenaline test. Roll one die, and add your **CONCENTRATION** to it. On a total of 5 or more: take **+2 {REASONABLE DOUBT}**; score 4 or less: take **-1 {REASONABLE DOUBT}**.

Once Spellcheck is securely tied up, the pair of you look around the attic. At the back of the space, you find a huge corkboard pinned with maps, photographs, scraps of newspaper article, and a dazzling web of red thread connecting it all. A big Thurstech logo is pinned near the heart of the chaos. You start carefully photographing everything. Take **+1 {MURDERBOARD}**.

With Spellcheck carefully stashed on the porch, and the police anonymously called to come and pick him up, you move on.

"Well, do you think we have enough to go on, or would you rather search Bright's workplace?" She-Hulk asks you.

"We've got enough." Turn to **252**.

"Better safe than sorry." Turn to **191**.

201

Despite Bessie's unearthly speed, She-Hulk manages to get a solid grab on her neck with one hand. A moment later, she has the vampire's jaw clamped in her other hand.

The Hellcow actually growls, then explodes into a cloud of fog that sinks into the underlying mist and vanishes.

She-Hulk sighs. "Typical." She looks around warily. "She won't have gone far." As if on cue, an eerie bovine cackle floats out of the night. "To me! Quick!" She-Hulk says.

You start forward, feeling a rush of air behind you as you begin running.

Somewhere up above, you hear a low, "Moo-oo-oo-oo-oo."

"We need some cover. I'll stay right behind you. Head for that oak tree."

"Right," you say, and walk briskly toward the big tree She-Hulk indicated.

Make an awareness test. Roll one die, and add your **CONCENTRATION** to it.

Score 5 or more: turn to **226**.

4 or less: turn to **268**.

202

The courtyard of the Vanguard compound is large and grassy, with several tall oak trees to provide shade, and unobtrusive tarmac paths leading here and there. It looks like it ought to contain a few dozen office workers lounging around comfortably reading or eating, but it's completely deserted.

A loud screaming whine startles you, and almost before you've had a chance to process it, a menacing black and red drone smashes out of the sky at you. It moves like lightning, 150 mph or more. Just in time, She-Hulk pushes you out of the way as it screams through the spot your head had just been in.

"Careful," she says, her eyes narrowed.

This is a quick fight. Roll two dice and add your **POWER**, and if you have any, your {DRONED} and your {NOBBLED}.

If the total is 12 or more, She-Hulk catches the drone and disables it. If you want a [Broken Drone], you may take it.

If the total is 11 or less, the drone explodes when she punches it. Take -1 POWER.

The walls of the compound are suspiciously thick. Are they hiding something?

To search the walls, turn to **47**.

To take cover against the main building, turn to **167**.

203

The other garden door leads to an attractive eating area with space for twenty or so, with a large marble staircase heading upstairs. A balcony overlooks the garden door, and there's a woman up there, watching warily. "Ah," she says, after a moment. "She-Hulk. I see now. Forgive me, I didn't recognize your real name. Come on up, both of you."

The woman leads you to a pretty little room, and pours some tea for you all. "My name is Caliburn," she says. "You may call me Exie. I was Sturm's second-in-command. Thank you for destroying that monstrosity, Ms Walters. It's been my warder for three months." Take **+1 {WHEELS WITHIN WHEELS}**.

"My pleasure," She-Hulk smiles. "Please, call me Jen. We were hoping you could tell us something about Sturm Vanguard's death."

The woman shudders, looking deeply saddened. "I didn't even realize it *was* a murder until a slender little popinjay of a man in an ugly suit barged in and had his shock-stick wielding thugs round up everyone. I have absolutely no idea who he was. We were informed it was going to be a suicide, the police would say that, and that anyone who even hinted differently would die horribly. I was ordered to keep a low profile and stay here so the company could tick over, on pain of death. The robot was programmed to destroy me if I tried to leave the grounds. Everyone else fled. Now that you've removed it, I'll definitely be following you out."

To ask about the murder, turn to **138**.

To ask about Sturm as a person, turn to **296**.

"Liquefy" is not the word closest in meaning to the other four. If you have both {MURDERBOARD} and {FILES} of 1, you can return to **252** and try again now.

If not, alas, you do your best to put together the pieces you have, but it doesn't make a whole heap of sense. Bright was very scared, that much is obvious. He's tracked more than a hundred deaths in the last three months that are clustered around six companies. These include both Thurstech and Omni and Grey. The root cause of his concern, however, seems to be the recent death of a famous tech visionary, Sturm Vanguard. At first Bright's notes read like mad rambling, but it quickly becomes clear that he was onto something.

To dig deeper into the six companies, turn to **233**.

To research Vanguard a bit further, turn to **238**.

Arcade sighs dramatically. "More empty threats, She-Hulk?" He stabs a key on his laptop. The room goes pitch black, and then all the screens start strobing, discordant sirens blare, and smoke starts billowing out from unseen vents. When you get the lights back on, Arcade is nowhere to be seen.

Over the next couple of hours, the police take over the scene and start dismantling the Murderworld. The Thing and Reed Richards get Chtylok transported back to where it belongs. Unfortunately, most of the VIPs did not survive. Even so, Ruby confirms that Arcade did not quite manage to assemble the system he was trying to build. "You were just in time," she says.

"What about you, Ruby?" She-Hulk asks, keeping her voice carefully neutral.

She snorts. "Oh, I was tempted. I could unify the six of us without even breaking a guideline, let alone the law. But you'd be there. Or Thor would, or Spider-Man, or Reed Richards, or Doom, or Kingpin, or... anyone, really. I don't want to rule the world, Jen. I genuinely don't. Far too much hassle."

ACHIEVEMENT: *By the Skin of Your Teeth.*

Final score: 2 stars.

The end.

206

The door shuts behind you as you come out into a pleasant garden courtyard, a large, grass-lawned space entirely within the main building. Decoratively arched flowerbeds are placed symmetrically to mark out a central circle of grass, and also run along the edges of the courtyard. Wooden benches provide some seating, but it does feel like there ought to be a few statues, or maybe a big tree or two.

Instead, there's a gigantic stompy death-robot, fifteen feet tall, with arms and legs three feet thick. The feet end in pads, but one arm terminates in a long, wickedly-sharp sword that sparkles with crackling energy, and the other in some sort of advanced laser cutter. There are gun-ports straight out of Japanese sci-fi movies in the shoulders, a glittering power core in its chest, and you wouldn't be at all surprised to discover that the eye-slits spit venom. It looks like an armored samurai warrior – one who is obsessed with Australian post-apocalyptic road movies and Finnish doom-metal bands.

She-Hulk twists her head back and forth, cracking her neck joints. You crouch in the doorway, trying to think unobtrusive thoughts. The robot surges forward, unreasonably fluid and graceful, swinging its laser-cutter like it was a cudgel.

Make a dodge test. Roll one die and add your **POWER**. If the total is 7 or less, She-Hulk is clipped and sent spinning off. Take **-1 POWER**.

Now make a focus test. Roll one die and add your **CONCENTRATION**. If the total is 7 or less, the robot follows up with a bruising kick to the face. Take **-1 CHARM**.

How's it going so far?

If you failed both tests, turn to **115**.

If you passed at least one of them, turn to **79**.

207

You rip a couple of sheets off your legal pad, and start exploring, putting scraps of paper down to mark your trail. It's really confusing and disorienting, but you keep your eyes on Jen as much as possible. The maze is not particularly difficult. If it wasn't for the mirrors, it'd be trivial. But wow, you're starting to really hate your reflection.

So how long does this take? Make a maze-solving test. Roll one die and add your **CONCENTRATION**. If the total is 10 or less, take **+1 {WATCHED}**.

Eventually, you come through to a section of normal wall containing three doors onwards. One shows a flower, one a painting, and one a statue.

For the flower door, turn to **255**.

For the painting door, turn to **264**.

For the statue door, turn to **175**.

208

"Anthony Bright's murder is littered with third-rate mercenaries like there was a hopeless villain convention in town or something," She-Hulk says. "The murder site was being watched by Bessie the Hellcow, for grief's sake. His home was booby-trapped, and his work had been mind-controlled. Before he was killed, he'd been putting together a dossier on a rash of unusual deaths at six tech companies: Thurstech, Omni and Grey, Tekeli Industries, Electronic Crafts, Shine Today, and AnxiousChimp. They started very soon after Sturm Vanguard's murder, and, yes, it *was* a murder. They'd set a huge killer samurai robot on his successor to keep her quiet."

Ruby thinks for a moment. "Flashy. Inefficient, expensive, and flashy. You're talking about a lot of resources sunk into this. I'm the only person at any of those companies who is genuinely ahead of the curve. Sturm had a brain, but his genius was in seeing connections and potentials. So maybe it's something to do with all six of us? Interesting. We're all leading companies, but no more so than twenty or thirty others."

"Vanguard was looking to invest in all of you, and no others," Jen says.

"Oh? I hadn't heard he was interested in AnxiousChimp or Shine. Sturm, you poor fool, what did you see? I know what Omni, Electronic Crafts, and AnxiousChimp have going on in their labs. I… No, I need more data. Whoever framed me, they had to know I'd not be here long. I don't like the edges of this though, Jen. Time could be critical. I'm going to need you to get me out on bail, today if possible."

Jen nods. "I'll do what I can."

It's unprofessional, but you have to ask:

"Surely someone as powerful as you are could just escape?" Turn to **241**.

"Is there anything you need while you're in here?" Turn to **80**.

209

It's a pleasant drive through the hills to Ruby's lonely estate. The walls are set back from the road a dozen yards, hidden away by a screen of trees and shrubbery. She-Hulk keys the entry code into the number-pad, and the wrought iron gates slide back silently. The mansion is a mile into the grounds. The perfectly kept gravel driveway winds tastefully through the trees, and flaming torches burn along its margins, one pair every twenty feet or so. The mansion itself is an imposing quasi-Gothic pile that looks like it should be crumbling in a damp New England forest rather than lounging in the Pacific sun. It looks like it matches the floorplans you got from the records office server, at least.

Ruby may have given up crime, but you get the feeling that she very much wants her guests to remember exactly who she used to be.

"Whoever 'they' are, they know we're here," Jen says. "There's no way that gate isn't monitored." Even so, you park up near the main door, next to a decorative fountain at the head of the driveway without any interference. She-Hulk gets out of the car, and nothing happens, so shrugging, she gestures for you to join her. "Which door?"

"The kitchens round the back." Turn to **10**.

"The pool area, on the left wing." Turn to **272**.

"The guest suite, on the right wing." Turn to **43**.

Arcade sighs dramatically. "So *violent*." Jen growls menacingly, and he shrinks back into his big chair. "Okay, okay," he says quickly. "You win. Don't kill me."

Over the next couple of hours, Arcade is carted away by the police, and work begins to start dismantling the Murderworld. The Thing and Reed Richards get Chtylok transported back to where it belongs. Unfortunately, most of the VIPs did not survive. Jen calls Ruby to have her come check over the computers, but she declines, and police forensic technicians impound the equipment for analysis.

Two days later, you're on a call to Jen in New York, to discuss you going there to see her offices, when she has to put you on hold for a minute for another line. When she comes back on, her voice is grim.

"That was Ruby. The police don't have Arcade. They don't even have a record of him. All the murdered VIPs have been scrubbed off the system. He *built* his system. She's going into hiding immediately. She recommends we do the same, right now."

There's a sudden crackle on the line. "I'm afraid it's too late for that," Arcade says in your ear. "Far too late."

ACHIEVEMENT: *It's Murderworld All The Way Down.*

Final score: 1 star.

The end.

As you start walking again, Jen nods. "What's important right now is that a programmer named Anthony Bright was shot to death just over there, and my client, Ruby, says she's being framed for it. It's plausible, but since she's a former supervillain, I want to be sure."

"I can understand that," you say.

"So, what do you make of Bessie's presence?"

"If I was framing a super villain, I might well want to drive off anyone who came digging."

Jen nods approvingly. "Exactly."

Take **+1 {REASONABLE DOUBT}**. Secondary qualities like these are always shown in **{CURLY BRACKETS}**, and start at 0. Since this is the first time you've come across it, your **{REASONABLE DOUBT}** is now 1. Keep track of them when they're mentioned, as they change how events unfold.

"So, where would you start looking?" she asks. "The precise murder site, that convenient thicket of trees over there, or the ornamental fountain?"

To check out the murder site, turn to **282**.

To start with the trees, turn to **237**.

To examine the area near the fountain, turn to **94**.

212

It's barely lunchtime, but the informant, a ratty little man named Earl, is already at the bar the judge's sister was snatched from. He gives the pair of you a calculating look as you come in, lingering on Jen a little more than is necessary. He starts turning around to leave, but she is already flashing a bank-note and looking at him, and he settles again. Over the course of an unpleasantly smarmy twenty minutes, while people around you gawp and whisper, Earl gets round to telling you that he saw the snatch, and that the woman was grabbed by a huge guy with an Australian accent. He does agree that someone like that probably stands out, but he's clearly wary of getting his nose bitten.

Make a persuasion test. Roll one die, and add your **CHARM**.

Total 8 or more: turn to **57**.

7 or less: turn to **95**.

213

She-Hulk staggers back from a particularly nasty hammer-blow to the temple, clearly dazed. While she's reeling, Walrus looks over at you and grins nastily. He surges forward, his hammer whistling. You duck...

Your world explodes in a very brief blaze of pain.

ACHIEVEMENT: *My Watermelon Impression*.

The end.

214

The attic trapdoor opens easily, and a metal staircase folds down with it. You go upstairs into a cavernous, dimly lit space. There are several anonymous shapes in the darkness but for a pleasant change, no stupid trap triggers.

Up ahead, someone starts laughing, a high-pitched, semi-hysterical noise that rolls on and on but still manages to be only the second-creepiest laughter you've heard in the last day or so.

"So you finally found your way through all my snares and sabotages," the man says. His speaking voice is as high and manic as his laughter, but the effect is spoiled by his thick New York accent. "I'm impressed."

"You really shouldn't be," She-Hulk says.

The man steps forward into a patch of light. He's tall and scrawny, and wearing a blue full-body outfit. There's a big red check-mark glued to his mask, running underneath his goggles. It sweeps up a full two feet over his head, wobbling slightly. The motif is repeated on the chest of his pointy-collared jacket, and again on his shoulders. "Tremble!" he demands. "Tremble at the sight of *Spellcheck!*" Take **+1 {WHEELS WITHIN WHEELS}**.

Jen stares at him for a long moment as he preens at the pair of you. "O-kay," she says slowly. "Look, we just need to ask you a couple of questions, and–"

She-Hulk ducks as Spellcheck flings something at her that lodges in the wall, vibrating. You realize it's a metal *S*, sharpened into a really ineffective throwing weapon.

"This isn't necess–" she begins, as a barrage of S-stars fly out of the darkness.

This is a fight, more or less.

"Definitely less," She-Hulk mutters.

Round one: roll two dice, add your **POWER**, and subtract your {DELAYED}, if any, to reflect Spellcheck's preparation time. If the total is 8 or more, you win the first round.

Round two: roll two dice, add your **POWER**, and subtract your {BITTEN}, if any, because She-Hulk has to make allowance for your slowed reactions. Yes, the snake was slightly venomous. But only slightly. If the total is 8 or more, you win the second round.

If you won both rounds, turn to **243**.

If not, turn to **51**.

215

You pass through the circle door into a very bright space. As your eyes start to adjust, you realize that you're surrounded. Before you can panic though, it becomes clear that you're looking at your own reflection in mirrors. Dozens of mirrors. Thousands of copies staring back at you both, wide-eyed, all around you, above you, below you… Infinite tunnels of your image flinch, cringing away. You turn to She-Hulk and laugh shakily, and your weak laughter booms back at you, rolling over and over, faster and then slower, on and on. It's… horrendous. Take **+1** {SHAKEN}.

Jen leans down to whisper in your ear. "We can be quiet." The horrible laughter dies down. "This is fine. Look over there, and there. Gaps and angles. It's just a maze of mirrors. Funhouse stuff. We got this."

"Yeah," you murmur. "Thanks."

"Only two ways out of a mirror maze," she suggests. "Breadcrumb trail or start smashing. You got a preference?"

"A trail." Turn to **207**.

"Smash it." Turn to **4**.

216

Jen stands up, abruptly. "I'm sorry. I thought I could do this, but I can't." She turns and walks out of the visiting room, leaving you to follow.

ACHIEVEMENT: *Just Too Much.*

The end.

217

The hotel is a crumbling heap on a decaying street in a deeply poor neighborhood. You park the car in front of a run-down but open bodega – *maybe* it'll still be there later – then walk the remaining blocks to the hotel. As you approach, you see a hefty, muscular man waiting for you on the steps up to the front door. He's hugely muscular, wearing some sort of tawny body and leg armor, with matching gauntlets and a silly, floppy-eared helmet, and he has a long chunky tail out the back of his armored trunks. Take **+1 {FLAT-FOOTED}**.

He lifts a massive hand in greeting as you approach. "G'day, Red."

"Hello, Brian," She-Hulk says. "I don't suppose we can have the judge's sister back peacefully, can we?"

"Strewth, mate, Buckley's chance," he replies, idiomatically.

He makes a sudden lunge, trying to grab Jen's suit. He's surprisingly fast. Make a dodge test. Roll one die and add your Power.

Total of 10 or more: turn to **2**.

9 or less: turn to **274**.

218

Despite Chtylok's best efforts to shake them off, She-Hulk and the Thing are still holding on to the sides of its head like a pair of angry novelty headphones. Its shoulders seem too massively over-muscled to let it reach up and pluck them off. The heroes are smashing at the side of its head, raining blows on what looks like its ear-holes.

Make a deafen test. Roll two dice, add your **POWER** and **CONCENTRATION**, and subtract your {WOBBLY}. If you have {OUCH!} of 1, add 10 to your total.

Get 20 or more: turn to **154**.

On a 19 or less: turn to **139**.

219

The abomination spots an opening, and uses a pseudopod to pull She-Hulk off-balance. Before she can recover, it slaps another thick, rope-like arm around her, then another and another. In moments, she's almost completely wrapped from head to toe. The pseudopods surrounding her thicken as it pushes more substance into them and you can see it start to squeeze. She yells in surprise, rage, and frustration.

Make a strength test. Roll one die, and add your **POWER** to it.

Get a 9 or more: turn to **267**.

8 or less: turn to **15**.

220

"I have to do this," you say.

Jen nods. "I understand. Be careful. Who knows, maybe you'll find your way back one day. Until then, goodbye."

Set {THE GREENEST DOOR} to 1, grab yourself a copy of *You Are (Not) Deadpool* (all good bookstores, comic shops, online retailers), and turn to entry **279** in that book. Farewell!

221

You hesitate a moment, then go to examine the robot close-up. It really is a magnificent piece of work. You expect to see recognizable components, in the joints at least – mechanical things like pistons or cogs or something – but the visible interior is as flowing and stylized as the exterior.

"It's very advanced," Jen says knowledgably. "Solidly built, too. It reminds of me of some of Tony's work. He'll probably want a look at it."

There's a piece of armor plating loose that you can grab, if you want to take a [Chunk of Robot].

To examine the garden, turn to **250**.

To leave the garden by the door you didn't come in through, turn to **203**.

222

Jen and Walrus exchange a few blows. The hammer is clearly hurting her when it hits, and Walrus's layers of blubber are blunting the force of her blows, but she's only looking annoyed, not worried. She steps in close to Walrus, elbows him square in the chest, and as he flails back, tries to get the hammer out of his grip.

This is a tricky fight. Round one: roll two dice, add your **POWER**, and subtract your {PENALTY}. If the total is 12 or more, you win the first round.

Round two: roll two dice, add your **POWER**, and subtract your {PENALTY}. If the total is 12 or more, you win the second round.

If you won both rounds, turn to **99**.

If you lost any rounds, turn to **284**.

223

The woods behind the café and visitor's lodge are surprisingly dense. You walk briskly along the flagstone path, quickly moving out of sight of anyone who might be watching. Despite your pace, it takes several minutes of winding through forest and around rocky hillside before you come to a junction.

Three paths lead onwards from this spot. One is grassy, somewhat overgrown, and snakes off into the woods. Another is concrete, utilitarian in its plainness. The third is more decorative, the flagstones becoming circular islands in a sea of woodchips, small ground-level lights set either side of it at regular intervals.

To take the grass track, turn to **61**.

To follow the concrete path, turn to **42**.

To try the attractive walkway, turn to **164**.

224

You follow the twists and turns of the maze, trying to ignore the faint scent of bone, until you find yourself stepping into a central space, next to the red-eyed skull. The light in its eyes flares, then dies away. As it does, the maze walls sink back into the floor. Take the ACHIEVEMENT: *Keep Turning Left*.

"That doesn't always work," Jen says, as if sharing a great secret. "It depends on the configuration."

"Huh?"

"Tell you later."

Three doors are now visible in amongst the bone walls. One shows a flower, one a painting, and the third a statue. Jen asks you to pick one, but if you like, you may take the [Mysterious Skull] with you before you go.

For the flower door, turn to **255**.

For the painting door, turn to **264**.

For the statue door, turn to **175**.

225

You walk up to the large glass panel and peer in. Either there's no sensibly sized room on the other side, or it's painted so pitch black that it swallows all the light coming from your bright room. It's impossible to know which. After a moment, you rap your knuckles on the glass. You're oddly relieved when no menacing shape swims out of the apparent void.

"I bet it's a missing entry," She-Hulk says. "After Bessie, I wouldn't put anything past them."

"A missing entry?"

She just shakes her head.

To poke around at the control panel, turn to **45**.

If you'd rather leave, turn to **206**.

226

The branches above you rattle for a moment, then again. You hear Bessie land softly, off to the right. She-Hulk immediately starts creeping round to the opposite side of the trunk, keeping her back to the tree. Sure enough, the Hellcow flashes out of the darkness to find She-Hulk stepping up to meet her. Bessie's crimson eyes flare up angrily, and the battle is on.

This is a boss fight!

Round one: roll two dice and add your **POWER**. If you have a [Terrible Stake] in your inventory, add 2. If the total is 8 or more, you win the first round.

Round two: roll two dice and add your **POWER**. Again, if you have a [Terrible Stake] in your inventory, add 1. If the total is 8 or more, you win the second round.

Round three: roll two dice and add your **POWER**. If you do have a [Terrible Stake] in your inventory, it just broke, so delete it. If the total is 8 or more, you win the third round.

If you won at least two rounds, turn to **181**.

If not, turn to **249**.

227

"Is there any hint of who might be behind this?" you ask.

"I've had a quick look, of course," Ruby says. "It's a Panama shell company held by a City of London shell company run by a Macau shell company, which was as far as I got before those idiots destroyed the hotel. The companies are all pre-made blanks that had been available for months, and the directors are all local cut-out lawyers. This is a government-level forensic accounting problem, and I don't have time to do it for you before the Expo opens tomorrow."

"We appreciate knowing that much," Jen says.

To ask what to expect from the Expo, turn to **266**.

Or, to head out to LA, turn to **150**.

228

She-Hulk falls back toward the altar, limping heavily, but manages to stay just out of Bi-Beast's reach. Just as you start to think she's in real trouble, she howls and rolls forward like a wrecking ball. Bi-Beast stumbles and, in a flash, She-Hulk's behind it, kicking it savagely in the back of the knee-joint. It topples forward, flat on its faces. She darts forward, heaves the massive marble altar up out of the floor, and snarling ferociously, smashes it down on the android's head with all her might.

Bi-Beast lets out a weirdly modulated shriek, and its body spasms. She-Hulk keeps on battering the monster, again and again. Eventually she stops, drops the stone altar and stands there shuddering for an endless moment. Take **-1 POWER** and **-1 CHARM**.

Eventually, she pulls her face back into its usual, pleasant expression. "Right. There are some doors down here," she says. "We should move on."

You join her, a little nervously, and see a couple of doors. One is stenciled with the icon of a coffee cup, other with a washbasin. "What do you think?" She-Hulk asks.

"I think we could use a hot drink." Turn to **299**.

"Freshening up sounds good." Turn to **26**.

229

The guard nods, and hands you a pair of lurid green pass-cards. "You know the way," he says.

Jen nods, and you drive through as the gate opens. Fortunately, visitor parking and the lobby are clearly signposted. You enter the sprawling lobby, passes prominently displayed. There's a lot of security around, but no one calls you out. Past a coffee concession, you spot a large pair of frosted glass doors with *RESTRICTED* stenciled across them. There's a card reader next to them, colored red. As you watch, a short-haired person in a pinstriped suit walks up and swipes a bright red card. The doors open, revealing a long corridor. The worker bustles through impatiently, and the doors close behind them. No one else appears to pay any attention.

"We could try to follow someone through," Jen says. "Or we could just make our own entrance."

"Slip in." Turn to **171**.

"Be direct." Turn to **131**.

230

You file into the ElectroCon main entrance, jostled all the way by eager fans. The entrance hall is huge, but so is the line to pick up badges, the line to check in, and the line to purchase a reservation. It looks like people just wandering in have to navigate all three of those lines, and the hall is already hot and kind of nasty.

Do you have {EXPO PASS} of 1? That's a pre-issued VIP +1 badge that will get the two of you into the games hall without any waiting, so turn immediately to **263**.

Otherwise, you have to put up with the soul-crushing wait.

Make a patience test. Roll one die and add your CONCENTRATION.

Total of 11 or more: you cope with only minimal annoyance, just take -1 CONCENTRATION.

10 or less: the whole process shreds your nerves – to a suspicious degree. Take -1 CONCENTRATION, -1 CHARM, and +1 {SHAKEN}.

Eventually you fight your way into the Expo proper. Signage is limited, and the con guide is absolutely no help at all, so you're not sure about the VIP area, but you can see directions to the games hall, the food court, and the information desk. Jen asks which you'd like to try first.

"The games hall." Turn to **263**.

"The food court." Turn to **54**.

"Information." Turn to **176**.

231

She-Hulk growls, and suddenly the charming, professional woman beside you is an absolutely terrifying being of pure rage. It feels like standing in the eye of a hurricane whirling with razor-sharp swords. The only reason you don't instantly cower for your life is that you're too terrified to move a muscle.

"*Eep*," Ringmaster manages, which is actually fairly impressive. Next to him, the little flame-haired man faints dead away. She-Hulk pounces, sending Ringmaster flying into a table full of computers.

Make an easy subdue test. Roll one die and add your **POWER** and **CHARM**.

10 or more: turn to **294**.

9 or less: turn to **177**.

232

Nothing changes visually, but as you stand there it's almosy like the floor has dropped away. You feel like you're perching on a tiny solid point, surrounded on all sides by an abyss. From Jen's confused expression, she feels it too. There's an immense sense of scrutiny, of some impossibly vast presence staring down into the deepest corners of your mind. It's horrible. Then the pressure just vanishes, and the world feels normal again. Take +1 {SPACE ALERT}.

"I guess we were… noticed," Jen says. You nod shakily.

Initially, the restricted section is a fairly normal-looking white tiled corridor – wider than usual maybe, and without windows or decoration, but not actually peculiar. Office doors are few and far between, and you decide not to risk them. As you explore, the corridor changes. After one junction, the lighting shifts to fluorescent floor strips, bright but casting odd shadows toward the ceiling. After another, there's a series of a dozen huge metal shutter-doors, ten yards apart. Just how big is this complex?

There has been quiet conversation and other sounds behind each door you've listened at so far. Despite this, you've not seen another living soul. It's eerie. Leading off from another junction, the corridor narrows, and the walls become brushed steel. You come to a pair of glass doors, and despite the murmurings that you can clearly hear coming from them, you can see that both rooms are empty of people. One of the rooms looks like a lab of some sort. The other one is smallish, and appears to hold some sort of big, free-standing glowing panel.

"Let's investigate," Jen suggests. "Which one?"

"The laboratory." Turn to **184**.

"The room with the glow." Turn to **276**.

233

Bright's notes on the six companies are fairly minimal – he seems to have been familiar enough with them that he felt no need to go into detail. He does list the names of them, however. You already know about Thurstech and Omni and Grey, but there's also Tekeli Industries, Electronic Crafts, Shine Today, and AnxiousChimp.

The heaviest losses have been at Tekeli Industries, twenty-four apparently-unrelated fatal accidents, random murders, and sudden suicides, all within the research department. That's almost a sixth of the department, if the corporate website is trustworthy. Take **+1 {NOT JUST A NUMBER}**.

Tekeli was the first company that Sturm Vanguard started openly showing interest in, followed swiftly by Thurstech. Ruby is involved in this mess, somehow. The Vanguard compound might have some answers.

To research Sturm Vanguard, turn to **238**.

To visit the compound, turn to **18**.

234

The tentacles look even less pleasant up close than they did from a distance. They're clearly organic, with an oily sheen, and they're approximately the color of cheap tinned spaghetti in tomato sauce. They don't smell, at least. You can't find any core or other central structure, but the individual filaments are not loose. Instead, they seem to branch and interconnect in a mystifying tangle. Whatever they are, you absolutely don't like them one bit.

If you want to properly look out of a window, turn to **93**.

If you'd rather progress on up the corridor, turn to **163**.

235

The guest bedroom is surprisingly small. There's a bed, a small dresser, and three large bookcases, and not much space left over. It's all blandly professional. Even the books are the sort of safe mass-market selection that interior designers buy by the yard.

You take a step, and a see-saw section of floor drops under your foot. She-Hulk instantly yanks you back – so she's the one that the bookcase falls on.

Make a trap! test. Roll one die and add your **POWER**.

Get a 7 or more: She catches it almost as soon as it start falling, and pushes it firmly back into place.

6 or less: Books topple out of the case, covering her in a pile of safely popular literature. She growls in irritation, and extracts herself impatiently. Take **-1 CHARM**.

She looks to the heavens with a long-suffering expression. "Why?"

You have no answer.

"I miss Renee," she says.

To search the spare room, turn to **66**.

To try the master bedroom, turn to **85**.

To look at the bathroom, turn to **271**.

236

The front porch is neatly painted, spotlessly clean, and completely devoid of any sort of homely clutter. The most interesting thing about it is the lone half-hearted strip of police tape across the front door. Jen gives the door an experimental try, then tugs briefly at the window nearby. "I'm not usually a fan of breaking and entering, but I really didn't want anyone knowing for sure that we were coming here," she says. "Not even Ruby – maybe especially not Ruby." You nod.

"So what do you think?"

To force the front door, turn to **193**.

To go through the curtained window, turn to **147**.

To try the back yard, turn to **44**.

237

The thicket is a way back from the path. There's not much to it, just a few trees in a clump, but it could certainly have been a place to watch the murder site from. glancing around, you spy a balled-up burger wrapper by a bush, probably no more than a couple of days old.

"Hmm," Jen says. "It could suggest a lurker. It could as easily be an office-worker's lunch though."

Make an awareness test. Roll one die, and add your **CONCENTRATION** to it.

On a 5 or more: You spot a square shape up in one of the trees, and investigate. It's a webcam, attached to a powered box. "That's seriously suspicious," Jen says. "Great find." Take **+1 {REASONABLE DOUBT}** and **+1 CONCENTRATION**.

4 or less: You poke around a bit, but it's just some trees. Time to move on.

"Where next?" She-Hulk asks.

"The murder site." Turn to **282**.

"The fountain." Turn to **94**.

"The lampposts." Turn to **269**.

238

Everyone knows Vanguard Technologies, Inc – or at least their products. They started with attractively designed smartphones, but quickly expanded out to include tablets, computers, televisions, watches, and just about anything else electronic. Now they control at least twenty percent of the consumer technology market. Sturm was only in his late thirties, charismatic, ruggedly handsome, and unfailingly cheerful, with a reputation for easy-going bonhomie.

Bright's notes clearly show a couple of near-miss accidents in the days before his death that really are quite suspicious. A balcony collapse, and a brake failure. Either could easily have proven fatal. The investigation into his suicide was perfunctory, at best. Take **+1 {SENSELESS}**.

Vanguard seems to be the first death, and Ruby was clearly linked with him. The compound is definitely worth checking out.

To research the six companies, turn to **233**.

To visit the compound, turn to **18**.

239

A rogue flurry of chain gun bullets ricochets off Ruby's shield, forcing you to duck behind a couch for several seconds. When you peek back up, she is closing on Big Wheel, lashing out toward his weapons systems with spikes of furious energy. Oort is a blur, zipping around the room so quickly that you can't really see him. Plasma blasts shoot out toward She-Hulk from all angles, and she ducks and weaves as she attempts to predict his movements enough to land a solid blow. Several fires are now burning aggressively around the destroyed lobby. Take **+1 {WAVES}**.

This is a hard fight.

Round one: roll two dice, add your **POWER** and **CHARM** to factor in Ruby's help, and subtract your **{LIT UP}** if any. If the total is 16 or more, you win the first round.

Round two: roll two dice, add your **POWER** and **CHARM** to factor in Ruby's help, and subtract your **{LIT UP}** if any. If the total is 16 or more, you win the second round.

If you win both rounds: turn to **40**.

If you lose at least one round: turn to **295**.

240

"That's a good call, actually," She-Hulk nods. "I don't entirely like the look of that hammer." She advances in a cautious crouch, her body tensed. Walrus advances, and somehow he doesn't look entirely foolish.

As he closes, he whips around in a spinning strike, using the hammer's extra momentum to drive himself forward at a surprising speed. Jen attempts to duck under the blow.

Make an evasion test. Roll one die, add your **CONCENTRATION**, and subtract your {PENALTY}.

One a 10 or more: turn to **99**.

9 or less: turn to **222**.

241

Ruby laughs, a rich, throaty sound. "Aren't you a darling little chaos puppy? Yes, I *could* walk through that wall in a moment – and instantly become guilty of a very serious federal crime. I haven't done anything wrong. I've become a hundred times wealthier and more powerful as a businesswoman than I ever managed before. It would be utterly irrational of me to threaten that."

Jen nods. "Yep. That."

You can ask if she needs anything by turning to **80**.

Alternatively, let She-Hulk ask about the bail situation by turning to **30**.

242

She-Hulk frowns. "There's definitely something not right with this whole affair. We need more information, but I have to say that so far, Ruby's version is making more sense." Take **+1 CHARM** and **+1 {SIMPATICO}** and the ACHIEVEMENT: *Suspicious Minds*.

"We need to find out who would want to frame her," she continues. "A competitor? An old foe? I just don't know. For now, we keep digging. Maybe we can confirm that Ruby was trying to recruit him. I have addresses for both the victim's home and his place of work up in the hills. Where should we start tomorrow?"

"Let's see what he had at home." Turn to **185**.

"His office might be interesting." Turn to **191**.

243

She-Hulk deflects the flying S-stars smartly, but the set of her shoulders makes you feel that she's getting annoyed. Spellcheck laughs again, sounding completely demented. You hear a magazine being clicked into place, and duck back a little further. He's got a huge, unwieldy industrial-looking gun-shaped device now.

"Please put that down before you hurt yourself," Jen says.

"You'd like that!" Spellcheck shouts, and cackles.

"Yes, I would!"

"Spike-Gun!" he shrieks.

She-Hulk sighs, and charges him.

This is an easy fight. Roll two dice, add your **POWER**, and subtract your {DELAYED}, if any.

On a 7 or more, turn to **200**.

6 or less, turn to **129**.

244

Chtylok was the last obstacle in Arcade's maze. You track him down to a comfortable boardroom not far from the arena. He's sat in the big executive chair you saw on the monitors, at the head of a very large meeting table. A score of shell-shocked tech executives are at the table with him, in front of various laptops. They all look pale and drawn and, in some cases, have obviously been injured.

As you walk in, Arcade stands and bows sarcastically, applauding. "Oh, well *done*," he says. "You beat the unstoppable monster. I'm going to have to kill that xenologist – but I suppose you must have some questions?"

"Only one," Jen says. "Are you coming quietly, or do I get to punch you?"

Add your **CHARM** and {SIMPATICO} together, and if the total is less than 10, turn to **260** now.

Still here? What is your {WAVES} score?

5 or more: turn to **285**.

4 or less: turn to **8**.

245

She-Hulk and Chtylok separate and circle each other warily. Even crouched over, the monster is still fifteen feet tall. It has apparently realized that she's not just some tasty morsel to devour, but it doesn't seem harmed. Jen darts forward, aiming to dash between its towering legs. It kicks out at her – and connects with a horrible meaty thud. Jen's flung clear out of the main arena to crunch painfully into the stone benches. Arcade cackles, delighted.

She-Hulk stands back up, grasping a very solid-looking stone bench that could probably seat six. She takes a moment to aim, then hurls it at Chtylok so ferociously that it blurs through the air.

Make an impromptu missile test. Roll one die, add your **CONCENTRATION**, and subtract your {WOBBLY}.

Get a 10 or more: turn to **140**.

9 or less: turn to **151**.

246

She-Hulk summarizes your investigation so far. Ruby seems baffled at the wasteful inefficiency of the things you've encountered, until Jen explains about the six companies and Sturm's death. Then she nods grimly. "Sturm must have seen something, a synergy between us. But I don't know what Tekeli Industries or Shine Today are actually up to. They're too secretive. I don't like the edges of this though. Time could be critical. I'm going to need you to get me out on bail, today if possible."

Jen nods. "I'll do what I can."

It's unprofessional, but you have to ask:

> "Surely someone as powerful as you are could just escape?" Turn to **241**.
>
> "Are you doing okay in here? Do you need anything?" Turn to **80**.

247

You pass through the square door into a big, empty grey room. There is a glow from weirdly sourceless ambient lighting, all the surfaces are exactly the same color, and the air is a little misty. Every time you take a step or make a movement, echoes rebound from all around. The effect is extremely disorientating.

Then the whispering starts. It could be coming from anywhere, and at first, you can't make it out at all. There's nothing else to focus on in here though, so you keep trying to make sense of it, and gradually the words become clear: "… worthless, disappointing, just useless. People would laugh at you if you were important enough to hurt, but you're not. You're nothing. Your efforts are dust, your dreams are husks, your hopes are futile. All you do is waste oxy–"

"SHUT UP!"

The words echo back from every direction, mocking, like a thousand strangers are laughing at you. Take **+1 {SHAKEN}**.

One wall lights up displaying the numeral "0". A moment later, three more words appear beneath it – "even?", "odd?", and "neither?".

What do you think the correct answer is?

Even? Turn to **16**.

Odd? Turn to **155**.

Neither? Turn to **41**.

248

"We need you on offence," you say. She-Hulk nods approvingly.

"Excellent," Ruby replies. "I prefer to lead." Take **+1 {SIMPATICO}**. She sprints off at an angle, toward the still-standing bits of the lobby's front wall.

A loud whine gives you a moment's warning, then Big Wheel is crashing back into the building again. This time, he ploughs straight through the gap and into the lobby proper. He's lucky the ceiling is high enough, frankly.

"A bit convenient," She-Hulk murmurs. She looks disgruntled.

The wheel pivots on the spot, turning so the chain guns are trained on She-Hulk.

A savage beam of crackling red energy smashes into the side of the wheel, spinning it like a top. You are surprised to see it's coming from the center of Ruby's head. Wow, impressive. The beam starts strobing, almost too fast to perceive, and Big Wheel's spin begins to accelerate. You can hear the engine of the wheel whining desperately, but he can't get any traction.

A blast of shining plasma jets past you, straight toward Ruby. Even five feet away, it's terribly hot. You panic for a moment, but she just sways lazily, and it goes through a window and out into the street. Jen growls and lunges forward at Oort, who has appeared nearby.

Oort is not particularly strong, but he is extremely fast, so this is a tough fight.

Round one: roll two dice and add your **POWER**. If the total is 13 or more, you win the first round.

Round two: roll two dice and add your **POWER**. If the total is 13 or more, you win the second round.

If you lost both rounds, take **-2 POWER** in plasma damage. That stuff is *hot*.

If you lost one or both rounds, turn to **122**.

If you won both rounds, turn to **186**.

249

It's difficult to follow the fight, but Bessie repeatedly forces She-Hulk back against the tree-trunk, pounding her with those razor-sharp hoofs. Unfortunately for the vampire, even her best blows leave little more than minor cuts. Finally Bessie backs off, hovering. She hisses once, a long sound full of irritation and spite, then retreats up into the air, fading slowly into the night sky as she flees.

"Is she gone?" you ask.

"Yes. She can't beat me, and now she's sure of it. She didn't survive four centuries of bovine undeath without knowing when to retreat."

ACHIEVEMENT: *Mooooo*. (Achievements are listed in the back of the book. Go check it off there if you like or, if this is an ebook, make a note of it somewhere safe.)

"I guess this is where I wake up, then?" you smile.

She-Hulk smiles sympathetically. "I completely understand your doubt, but you *are* awake. This is the real world. Bessie genuinely is an ancient vampire cow, and she did just attack us." She pauses for a moment. "It's been a weird day."

"Right," you say hesitantly. "Weird. Sure."

"Look, the quick version is, I'm considering a new client. I don't have offices in California, so I need local help: you. But I'm also between permanent paralegals, so you can consider this an extended interview. That's why I asked for your input on how to approach Bessie. Whether you know it or not, you've got someone extremely special looking over your shoulder. I'll do my very best to keep you safe – and my best is pretty good. We can make a real difference together. Are you in?"

You nod. If you are really awake, this just became the best day ever. "Yes, Mi– Jen. All in. Weirdness or not."

She smiles. "Great! I think we've got a few moments. Do you want the background on the client now?"

"Yes, please." Turn to **192**.

"May I catch up later?" Turn to **211**.

250

The garden is an interesting spot, when you take a metaphorical step back and actually think about it as a constructed space. Attractive and convivial, yes. Quite charming, even. Slightly showy – it makes a statement about how much room there is to waste here – but regular and well-balanced, and without any excesses of frivolity. Oh, except for the gigantic, stompy, broken death-robot of course.

You feel, for the first time, that Sturm Vanguard might actually have been quite interesting to know. Take +1 {WHEELS WITHIN WHEELS}.

> To examine the broken robot, turn to **221**.
> To leave the garden by the door you didn't enter through, turn to **203**.

251

The trapdoor down into the cellar really is unlocked. You go down into the dingy darkness, using your smartphones for some light. Take **+1 CONCENTRATION**.

This probably isn't a murder basement, but it could certainly pass for one if you moved the empty storage shelves out. Rough concrete isn't automatically creepy, but below a house like this, it feels like an ugly afterthought. Cheap wooden stairs lead upwards out of the darkness, and there's nothing to look at, so you head toward them. Take **+1 {REASONABLE DOUBT}**.

Now make a trap! test. Roll one die, and add your **POWER**.

Total of 6 or more: She-Hulk springs to the side as a torrent of foul-smelling slime sprays up from a well-disguised grille in the floor.

5 or less: The vile, sticky mess catches you both by surprise, coating you from head to toe in gross muck. It takes for*ever* to scrape off, and afterwards you still both look like the victims of a bad 80s game-show. Take **-1 CHARM** and **+1 {DELAYED}**.

Now you can continue on, even more warily.

To head up to the dining room, turn to **52**.

To search the kitchen, turn to **156**.

252

Jen is staying at a pleasant business hotel downtown, and the two of you set up in the large, mostly deserted café-bar to go over the information you've retrieved. Everyone's far too polite to stare openly, so instead they stare surreptitiously, which is actually somehow worse. "You get used to it," Jen says, glaring at your expression. "It's never nice, but, well... I *do* stand out, and people are hard-wired to be curious and cautious about people who stand out. And I get pestered by far fewer aggressive dudebro types nowadays, so it's a net plus."

Making sense of the information is going to take some time – it's not a report, after all, it's more like a set of cryptic notes – but one thing leaps out at you immediately. There have been a *lot* of odd deaths recently, and Bright was deeply concerned about them.

This is a puzzle that mimics the challenge of trying to put the pieces together. Consider the words *Determined, Comportment, Scene* and *Collection*. Which of the following words is most closely associated with them?

ESTABLISH: turn to **149**.

LIQUEFY: turn to **204**.

DROP: turn to **143**.

SET: turn to **96**.

253

She-Hulk leads you round the side of the building, to the far end. "This should be safe to go through without collapsing the place or hitting someone with rubble."

While you're still processing that, she casually punches the wall, which collapses, then saunters into the Barn. You follow, not a little awed, to find yourself inside an office restroom. Jen dusts herself off, then you both exit into the main office. There's a maze of high-tech workstations, dozens of them, comfortably slotted in with snack machines, foosball tables, beanbags, arcade machines, and other tech toys. The main door is at the far end.

A pack of people are gathered at the far side of the office, forty or more of them. Their faces are completely expressionless, but they are clutching improvised weapons – chunks of heavy-looking metal pipe, mostly. Take **+1 {REASONABLE DOUBT}**.

Make an observation test. Roll one die, and add your **CONCENTRATION** to it.

Get a 7 or more: there's a fire alarm on the wall next to you and acting on instinct, you pull it. A siren immediately blares, and the pack of people turn around, head to the main door, and leave. Turn directly to **145**.

6 or less: an intercom crackles, and a voice says "Intruders are not one. They do not make sense." The pack snarl with identical expressions of rage and sprint at you.

This is a simple fight, because the pack are spread out by having to wind their way through the office to reach you.

Roll two dice and add your **POWER** and, if you have any, your **{TRANSFORMED}**. If the total is 10 or more, you win.

If you won, turn to **145**.

If you lost, turn to **101**.

254

She-Hulk asks Ben how things are going, and his smile gets even wider. "I ought to make some wisecrack, but honestly, it's great. Alicia is just incredible, you know? Married life is good, Jen. It's the happiest I've ever been. I never imagined a big lug like me could ever find anyone, let along someone so amazing, but if I can do it… Keep your eyes open, is all I'm saying."

She smiles at him. "We'll see. I'm really happy things are good for you. It's been a rocky road, I know."

"No green pastures, that's for sure."

"A lumpy ride, you could say."

The Thing splutters for a moment, then they're both laughing. "It's good to see you, girl," he manages.

To fill Ben in on the current situation, turn to **275**.

To ask why he's come out west, turn to **283**.

255

The flower door leads you into a small stone room. Small streams run in grooved channels along the base of the walls, which are festooned in flowering vines. Morning glories, maybe? You're no expert. There's a stone plinth in the middle of the room, with a pair of pewter goblets on it, filled to the brim with liquid. It *might* be water. It's hard to tell.

"Choose," booms a voice from the ceiling. "Choose and drink."

"Or?" asks Jen.

"Choose," repeats the voice.

Jen shrugs at you. "I'm not particularly susceptible to poison. How obedient are you feeling?"

If you want to pick a goblet for her to drink, pick either "left" or "right", then turn to **76**.

If you want to tip the liquid on the floor, turn to **160**.

256

She-Hulk falls back to the altar, staying just out of Bi-Beast's reach. Just as you start to think she's going to hamper her movements, she rolls forward like a wrecking ball. Bi-Beast stumbles over her, and in a flash, Jen's behind the fiend, kicking it savagely in the back of the knee. It topples forward, flat on its faces. She darts forward, heaves the massive marble altar up out of the floor and, snarling ferociously, smashes it down on the android's head with all her might.

Bi-Beast lets out a weirdly modulated shriek, and its body spasms. She-Hulk slams it down again and again, until Bi-Beast's body has fallen still and silent. She drops the altar and stands there shuddering for a moment.

Eventually, she pulls her face back into its more usual, pleasant expression. "OK. There are some doors down here," she says. "We should move on."

You join her, just a little nervously, and spot a couple of doors. One is stenciled with the icon of a coffee cup, and other with a washbasin.

"What do you think?" She-Hulk asks.

"I think we could use a hot drink." Turn to **299**.

"Freshening up sounds good." Turn to **26**.

257

You follow the twists and turns of the maze, trying to ignore the faint scent of bone, until you find yourself trapped in a block whose entrance sealed behind you as you entered. Jen rolls her eyes, and starts kicking the bone walls to shreds. Before long, all the maze walls are gone. Take **+1 {WATCHED}**.

There are three doors onward. One shows a flower, one a painting, the third a statue. Jen asks you to pick one.

For the flower door, turn to **255**.

For the painting door, turn to **264**.

For the statue door, turn to **175**.

258

You were expecting the home theater to be some sort of movie room, but no, it is in fact a traditional theater, complete with a generous stage, floodlights, extensive curtains, and a sprawling backstage area. A quick look at the rows of seats suggests room for more than a hundred audience members.

For a moment, you're sure you see someone sitting in the front row, a dark-haired woman, but you blink and she's gone. Jen doesn't seem to have noticed her.

"The far door over there leads to the snack bar, or we can try the casino," Jen says.

For the casino, turn to **161**.

For the snack bar, turn to **259**.

The snack bar is oddly tatty – there's a dozen different vending machines, several offering options like fresh pizza and lasagna, and a self-service food area that is currently empty. Most of the vending machines look to have been cleared out too. There are no coin slots or prices. What does grab your attention is a sturdy looking oak door with a red light above it. It has a big keypad to one side – the entry to the secure suite.

You head over there. Jen tries the code Ruby gave her, but unsurprisingly, it doesn't work.

This is a puzzle! Look at the following numbers: 63, 67, 75, 87, 83.

One of them is the odd one out. Turn to the entry equal to the number you pick, but if the first words you see are not "This is the odd one out!", turn to **195**.

Alternatively, you can take a penalty and bypass the puzzle by turning to **29**.

260

Arcade sighs dramatically. "*Such* violence." Jen growls menacingly, and he shrinks back into his big chair. "Okay, okay," he says quickly. "You win. Don't kill me."

Over the next few hours, Arcade is carted away by the police, the Thing and Reed Richards arrange an airlift to get Chtylok back where it belongs, the Murderworld is dismantled, and the final body count is tallied. Many of the VIPs survived, but many others did not.

A week or so later, you're in New York visiting Jen's office to discuss your future when a computer monitor suddenly flicks on to show Ruby's head. "Hi," she says. "Have a look out the window!"

Heart sinking, you do so. Down the block, a series of electronic billboards switch over to show Ruby miming blowing you a kiss.

"It's a brave new world," she says, from the monitor. "*My* world," she adds, her voice now coming from the mobile phone in your pocket. "And I couldn't have done it without you. Be good now. I'll be watching."

All of the electronics in the office power down and, all across the city, the lights start to go out.

ACHIEVEMENT: *Rubygeddon.*

Final score: 0 stars.

The end.

261

The stairs up to the next floor are wooden slats built into the wall. It looks very chic, but you can't help feeling that railings are a good policy.

"How would you trap these stairs?" She-Hulk asks.

You consider it. "Have them retract into the wall, triggered halfway up."

"I like it. But that seems ambitious compared to the traps we've seen so far."

"Hm. Saw through a couple of steps? Or oil them to be slippery?"

She nods. "I think the main point is, who cares?" She puts a mighty arm around you and jumps, soaring effortlessly to the top of the staircase to land with a *thud*.

You glance back to see a step fall downwards, dangling from a hinge next to the wall, and shrug. Close enough.

There are several rooms to check upstairs.

To try the master bedroom, turn to **85**.

To examine the guest bedroom, turn to **235**.

For the spare room, turn to **66**.

262

As you approach, the exhausted woman does her best to stand up straight and seem attentive. She even manages a smile of sorts, but her eyes just look beaten. "How can I help?" she asks.

"I'm going to be honest," Jen says. "I'm going to offer you money to let us in to the VIP area, but I prom–"

"I suspect that's a bad idea for you," the woman says.

"I know."

She looks at Jen more closely. "Ohh. Wow. I'm… Wait, I'm in real danger, aren't I."

"I'm afraid so."

"OK. Here's the card. Just swipe. It's amazing, an honor, my privilege, gotta dash, so long, bye bye."

"Wait!"

The woman pauses, mid-turn. "Er, yeah?"

Jen passes her some folded cash. "Have a cab and a meal on me. Thank you."

The woman beams shakily at her. "You really *are* the best." Then she's away, all but sprinting into the distance.

Jen smiles at her back. "She's going to get her own book one day, mark my words." She swipes the card and the door opens. You walk through into a small stretch of beige corridor. There are three frosted glass doors at the other end, one directly ahead and the other two set in the walls opposite each other. One is red, one is green, the third blue.

"I've got a bad feeling about this," Jen says. "Which door would you pick?"

"Red." Turn to **194**.

"Green." Turn to **178**.

"Blue." Turn to **298**.

263

The games hall is so thronged that you can barely move around. Garish stands occupy much of the floor-space. They are freestanding structures the size of a decent townhouse that bristle with display screens, advert hoardings, barely-clad women, and smirking PR drones.

The crowd seethes all around them along the grid of aisles, and despite the loudspeaker stacks, the excited chatter drowns out everything. It's hard to even think, let alone learn anything useful.

High up on a stand across the way, someone in a dark hoodie is watching you closely. The vibes they're putting out are all wrong. You start to head over toward them, but they calmly turn around and vanish into the background. Take +1 {WATCHED}.

This hall is way too busy to get anything useful done.

To try the food court, turn to **54**.

To try information, turn to **176**.

To wander the complex hoping to spot something, turn to **88**.

264

The portrait door leads you into a well-lit hallway, off-white and modern in style. One side of the wall is lined with tall paintings, floor to ceiling, jammed up against each other. The art is Romantic, oil paintings of old-fashioned people painted realistically, but in emotionally overcharged or fantastical situations. None of the images look familiar, but it's undoubtedly talented work. The hallway ends in a blank wall – no obvious way onward.

Then the heads in the paintings all turn to look at you, which is surprisingly freaky. How are your nerves doing? If your {SHAKEN} is 5 or more, take -1 CHARM and -1 CONCENTRATION.

Every eye is watching you. Every mouth opens simultaneously, and the paintings all speak with a perfectly coordinated polyphonic voice. It's a surprisingly unpleasant effect. "I have been tomorrow and will be yesterday," they say. "What am I?"

To try to answer, turn to **277**.

To destroy the paintings, turn to **136**.

265

Chtylok thrashes its head around, trying to shake both She-Hulk and the Thing off. Although Jen manages to keep her grip, the Thing is flung across the arena. He lands badly, and lies there on the sand, groaning. She-Hulk looks like she's faltering, but she desperately pounds at the side of the monster's head, trying to strike at its crazed red eyes.

Make a blinding test. Roll two dice, add your **POWER** and **CONCENTRATION**, and subtract your {WOBBLY}.

Get a 21 or more: turn to **139**.

20 or less: turn to **22**.

266

"What can we expect from the Expo?" you ask.

"It's a trap," Jen says. "Obviously."

"Quite," Ruby says. "The ElectroCon VIP list is suspiciously narrow, and the list of facilities and events organized for VIPs is far more vague than it should be. The real kicker is that, up until four months ago, the keynote lists and other promotional blurbs were significantly different. The company that runs the event was bought out, and there was a major shake-up. I initially assumed Vanguard was quietly trying to woo us. I think it's clear now that this is not the case."

To ask who is behind the Expo, turn to **227**.

To head out to LA, turn to **150**.

267

With a wild yell, She-Hulk flings herself straight into the mass of the abomination. It engulfs her and she vanishes. Ah.

You're beginning to wonder exactly how badly things have gone when the thing suddenly shudders, and eerie purple energies start crackling over its surface. It starts thrashing around wildly, the eye rolling around crazily. You can see the edges of its form begin to fray.

Make a resilience test. Roll one die and add your **POWER** and **CONCENTRATION**.

If you have {ILLUMINATED} of 1, or if the total is 15 or more, take **-1 CHARM**.

If the total is 14 or less, take **-2 CHARM**, **-2 CONCENTRA-TION**, and **-2 POWER**.

In less than thirty seconds, the abomination has dissolved into huge, revolting pool of sticky ooze. She-Hulk is standing in the middle of the revolting pool, looking annoyed, slimy, and thoroughly grossed out. ACHIEVEMENT: *Smashing*.

To examine the remains and the archway, turn to **102**.

To examine the computer equipment, turn to **116**.

268

The branches above you rattle for a moment, then a second time. You hear Bessie land softly, off to the right. She-Hulk frowns and gestures you forward a step, moving behind you with her back to the tree.

The Hellcow flashes out of the darkness on your left, lunging for you. Jen steps between you. You can see that her balance isn't quite right. Bessie's crimson eyes flare up angrily, and the battle is on.

This is a boss fight!

Round one: roll two dice and add your **POWER**. If you have a **[Terrible Stake]** in your inventory, add 2. If the total is 10 or more, you win the first round.

Round two: roll two dice and add your **POWER**. If you have a **[Terrible Stake]** in your inventory, add 1. If the total is 9 or more, you win the second round.

Round three: roll two dice and add your **POWER**. If you have a **[Terrible Stake]** in your inventory, it just broke, so delete it. If the total is 8 or more, you win the third round.

If you won at least two rounds, turn to **181**.

If not, turn to **249**.

269

"The lampposts?" She-Hulk says. "Interesting. Let's do it."

The two of you walk along the paths near the murder site slowly, scanning the lamps and their posts. On top of the fourth pole, you spot what you were expecting – an unmistakable security camera. What's more, it's clearly broken.

"That's good thinking," Jen says approvingly. "Let's check it out." She leaps straight up in the air, easily clearing the top of the lamppost, and on the way back down, she casually reaches out and takes the broken camera. She lands back beside you with a solid *thud*, already studying the device. "It's been shot out," she says. "Small caliber, like the wounds on the victim. I saw several other cameras from up there too. Every ten posts. All the ones nearby are out."

"Maybe Ruby didn't want to be filmed," you say.

"Maybe. But she's a computer genius, not a sharpshooter. She'd just hack the footage. This is definitely suspicious." Take **+1 {REASONABLE DOUBT}** and **+1 {WHEELS WITHIN WHEELS}**.

What is your **{REASONABLE DOUBT}** level now?

3 or more: turn to **242**.

2 or less: turn to **103**.

270

The Thing doffs his fedora and looks around meaningfully. A young guy walking past stops, does a double take, and says, "Nice cosplay, guy. You need to work on the color, but it's decent work. Talk to your girlfriend there, she's got the paint right." Then he smirks and moves on.

"See what I'm up against?" Ben grumbles. "You'd have trouble finding Galactus in this crowd. There could be twenty capes within fifty yards."

To ask whether he knows where the VIP area is, turn to **34**.

To head into the Expo, turn to **230**.

271

The bathroom is about what you expected – huge and attractively tiled, with a vast mirror and a claw-footed ceramic bathtub. Fluffy white towels the size of an entire bedspread hang from hooks on the wall. Bright surely had to use this room, but there's little sign of it.

One exception is the strangely cheap bottle of shampoo. You understand he really didn't care about this house, just used it like a hermit crab in a shell, but he would have had to deliberately visit a dollar store to get hold of that muck. Odd.

There is a cupboard under the sink, and maybe there's something under there, but honestly, the trapdoor up into the attic is a much more tempting prospect.

To go up to the attic, turn to **214**.

To search the master bedroom, turn to **85**.

To check the guest bedroom, turn to **235**.

272

The pool area is quite charming, and obviously set up for swimming more than partying. On the side near the mansion is an open-air weight training space, canopied to keep off the sun. Inside, through large, open French doors, is a suite of fitness machines. The man standing in those doors is significantly taller and more muscular-looking than most all-in wrestlers. He's wearing a natty off-the-shoulder leotard the same golden brown color as his hair, and he has chunky studded metal cuffs on his wrists. In other company, he'd look quite intimidating.

Jen nods to herself. "Bruto. But of course."

The big man snarls, revealing white tombstone teeth, snatches up a massive dumbbell bristling with weights, then flings it straight at her head. Rude!

Make a reflex test. Roll one die and add your **POWER**.

Get a 6 or more: turn to **104**.

On a 5 or less: turn to **125**.

273

Your research made it clear that the compound's deliveries come by self-driving unmanned truck. Bright made careful notes on timing, and there are several deliveries a day. You could feasibly intercept one, force the door, and have the truck deliver you.

If you have {LEISURELY RESPONSE} of 1, there's a police cruiser following you at a discreet distance. Hijacking a drone truck is not going to be an option. Turn back to **18** now and choose something else.

Otherwise, you quickly come up with a plan cunning where you both get in the road in front of the truck, and when it stops, Jen pulls a door open and hold the truck still until you're both in. Take **+1 CONCENTRATION**.

Now make a cunning plan test. Roll one die and add your **CONCENTRATION** to it. If the total is 8 or more, you stop the truck successfully, and it takes you inside. Turn to **202**.

If not, it's back to square one.

> If you have {FOOD TRUCK} of 1 and want to try talking your way onto a sandwich van, turn to **97**.
> To scale the wall, turn to **119**.

274

Jen sways back as the huge man grabs at her, badly ripping her suit. Take **-1 CHARM**.

She growls and kicks him in the chest. He leaps out of

her way, twisting to impact the wall across the street feet first. He then springs off it somehow, cheering wildly, and jumps back to land on a hotel balcony several floors up.

"Kangaroo, of all idiots," she mutters. "This is so undignified." She-Hulk leaps, sailing up toward Kangaroo's position as he hops over his balcony and falls.

Make an aerial maneuvers test. Roll two dice, add your **POWER** and **CONCENTRATION**, and subtract your {FLAT-FOOTED}, if any.

On a 17 or more: turn to **135**.

16 or less: turn to **9**.

275

It takes several minutes just to give the Thing a cut-down version of events. Once She-Hulk finishes, he sits there for a several seconds, digesting it all. "I dunno, Jen. You sure Ruby can be trusted?"

"I trust her intelligence and self-interest," Jen says. "She's built a genuinely legitimate world-class business, and it's going from strength to strength. She's already earned a fortune. It would be really dumb to risk that, and she's very nearly as brilliant as Reed. Whoever is behind this wanted her out of the way for this convention."

"That's worrying on different levels. Sounds like Reed might be on to something."

To catch up with Ben personally, turn to **254**.

To ask why he's come out west, turn to **283**.

You enter the smaller room. The walls and floor are bare concrete that's been given a quick coat of whitewash. As you get closer to the glow, you realize that it is a perfectly flat circle seven feet across – a shimmering portal. It is absolutely obvious that it leads to a different reality. You think about it for a moment.

"That car, though," Jen says. "Don't say I didn't warn you."

To head out of this reality, turn to **28**.

To stay here and explore the lab, turn to **184**.

You ponder the riddle for a while – not long, between the two of you, but is it swift enough? Let's find out.

Make a puzzle test. Roll one die and add your **CONCENTRATION** and your {PUZZLER}, if any. If the total is 8 or less, you are noticed from afar – take **+1** {WATCHED}.

"I am 'today,'" you say. "Yesterday, I was tomorrow. Tomorrow, I will be yesterday." ACHIEVEMENT: *Riddled*.

Several paintings slide smoothly up into the ceiling to reveal a pair of doors. They have plaques this time. One says *Temple*, the other says *Pool*.

For the temple, turn to **166**.

For the pool, turn to **62**.

278

You really trounced Kangaroo, huh? Sure, feel good about that for a moment. He did manage to mutate himself some extra strength and toughness in the end, even if he is still a bit of a drongo. Not bad for an interior decorator from Cairns. Take the ACHIEVEMENT: *Bouncing Matilda*.

While Jen's tying him up, a [Sinister Medallion] falls out of his pocket. You may take it. While it is in your inventory, it increases your **CONCENTRATION** by 2. Who knows? It might even do other things as well. But hey, if you can't trust a Sinister Medallion, what can you trust?

For now, you can let She-Hulk take a breather, or start interrogating Kangaroo.

For a breather, turn to **124**.

To talk to the Australian, turn to **168**.

279

Welcome from *You Are (Not) Deadpool*! She-Hulk is in the middle of a deadly web, and she definitely needs some expert guidance.

Set your **POWER, CHARM, CONCENTRATION** and {WAVES} to 5 each. Cross off all of your equipment.

Now, do you have {THE GREENEST DOOR} of 1?

Yes: that was a long, strange trip, but you're home. Take the *achievement: Dazzled* and turn back to the portal room at **276**.

No: turn to **1**, but ignore the stat instructions in the entry you choose to visit from there.

280

Before we continue with the adventure, let's set up the stats for your team of She-Hulk and the Paralegal. There are three core stats, **POWER**, **CHARM**, and **CONCENTRATION**. You remember that from the introduction, which you absolutely read, right?

Power represents She-Hulk's current strength, agility and resilience. Very helpful for punching things, which is definitely a talent of She-Hulk's, along with hurlings things, leaping over things, smashing things, and all manner of other tasks you'll encounter in time.

Charm is a measure of how eloquent and persuasive other people consider She-Hulk to be at the time. It rises and falls with her patience level, and it can be affected by physical effects and events that might impact other people's perceptions. Being covered entirely head to toe in reeking ectoplasmic goo is bad for your **CHARM**, for example.

Concentration, finally, indicates your team's current level of mental ability. It's handy for solving problems, spotting objects that are out of the way or hard to notice, and thinking up clever solutions on the fly. You'll still have to solve the puzzles in this book on your own, however.

Your core stats will change repeatedly over the course of your adventure, so you'll need to keep track of them on a piece of paper or something similar. You start with **POWER** of **2**, **CHARM** of **2**, and **CONCENTRATION** of **3**.

Right, on with the fun...

• • •

Grinning like a mad person, you suggest, "Does she have any weaknesses?"

"Of course. Fire, sunlight, religious symbols wielded by a true believer, garlic, stakes. I don't suppose you're strongly religious?"

You shake your head.

"Too bad." She jumps straight up without warning, snaps a branch off a tree, and lands back on the path. "Wooden stake. Sort of." She grins fiercely at Bessie. "Ready to dance, Hellcow?"

Add a [Terrible Stake] to your inventory.

"Moo." Bessie flickers forward, faster than the eye can follow, a smear of black and brown against the night. Then she's right up in She-Hulk's face, those glittering red eyes boring into Jen's. "Mooooooooo," she says, suddenly quiet and weirdly suggestive.

Make a willpower test. Roll one die, and add your **CHARM** and **CONCENTRATION** to it. What's the result?

Get a 7 or more: turn to **173**.

6 or less: turn to **86**.

281

It takes a few minutes for the jail staff to bring Ruby to the phone. The call is on speaker. You hear a clatter, and then her voice. "Hello, Jen."

"We had to slap down the Circus of Crime, but we've got your file," She-Hulk says. "It's more than enough. This whole arrest is insane. A drunk teenager could get you off this one, frankly."

"Quite. So why *did* I call you?"

Jen thinks for a moment. "You must know this is no threat. But there's a lot of ruthless money behind this. A serious attempt to frame you would be less pathetic. You're just supposed to be distracted for a week."

"Go on," Ruby says, approvingly.

"Someone recognizes you as dangerous opposition. That didn't stop them however, and they hired Bessie, Ringmaster, and other second-tier talents. So there's most likely a powered criminal behind this, and they win this any day now. Which suggests–"

"That I'm not going to like it, this needs to be stopped now, and I need someone in my corner who is both a top-flight hero and who can get me off the bench quickly. Exactly." Take **+1 {SIMPATICO}**.

Jen promises to have Ruby out ASAP, and hangs up.

To research Ruby's case in more detail, turn to **133**.

To go arrange Ruby's bail, turn to **128**.

282

The exact murder site is off the path, roughly equidistant from the thicket of trees and the fountain. The ground is quite churned up, but despite the low light, there are still some clear footprints that show someone was here in a pair of stylishly-heeled boots, and someone with bigger feet was here in sneakers. There are also a couple of spots where shell casings could have been first embedded in the soil and then removed.

"Does the client wear boots?" you ask.

Jen nods. "Good. Yes, she certainly has, and before you ask, yes, the police retrieved casings."

"So the site is consistent."

"Seems like it. No clear struggle, shots fired, appropriate footprints, and it fits with the body. But…"

Make a profiling test. Roll one die, and add your **POWER** and **CONCENTRATION** to it.

Get an 8 or more: "I just don't see Ruby shooting someone. She has quicker, less identifiable ways of killing." Take **+1 {REASONABLE DOUBT}** and **+1 POWER**.

7 or less: "No, never mind."

"Let's move on," she says. "Where next?"

"The trees." Turn to **237**.

"The fountain." Turn to **94**.

"The lampposts." Turn to **269**.

"Reed was doing some sensor work yesterday, and whatever he found left him stressed and snappy. I mean, more than usual. There are some very anomalous readings coming out of this conference center, and he really doesn't like it. After a load of double and triple checks, he decided that someone had to investigate it, and naturally Johnny was nowhere to be seen, and Reed and Sue turned to me with that glint in their eye that says I just got volunteered. So here I am, surrounded by screaming teenagers and considering the life choices that brought me here."

"I know that feeling," Jen says. "I mean, Kangaroo? Damn."

To ask about the sensor data, turn to **100**.

To ask if Ben has any theories, turn to **132**.

To ask what he knows about the Expo, turn to **142**.

She-Hulk shoves Walrus away, ruining his balance. She follows up with a punch, but he fends it off with the hammer, then lashes a blow at her neck. She steps back, and he flings himself at her, hammer smashing into her knee. She curses and staggers back, and to your surprise, Walrus turns and runs. He's fast, too. By the time She-Hulk is moving freely again, he's already left through the door through which you came in.

Jen thinks about it for a moment, then shakes her head. "Annoying as that was, he's not the priority. Our spider will be at the center of this web. We should press on."

The far end of the room opens up into a changing area with a shower unit, beyond which you see a couple of doors. One is stenciled with a coffee cup icon, the other with a washbasin.

"What do you think?" She-Hulk asks.

"I could use a coffee." Turn to **299**.

"How about the washroom?" Turn to **26**.

285

Arcade sighs dramatically. "More empty threats, She-Hulk?" He presses a key on his laptop. The room goes pitch black, then all the laptop screens start strobing, discordant sirens blare, and smoke starts billowing out. The prisoners completely freak out. When you get the lights back on, Arcade is nowhere to be seen.

Over the next couple of hours, the surviving tech gurus and privacy campaigners are taken to nearby hospitals for emergency treatment, trauma counseling, and/or medical examination, as appropriate. Ruby comes over to take a look at Arcade's computer systems, and confirms that he did not manage to assemble all the code he required. "You were just in time," she says. "He was still trying to pry vital modules out of Tekeli and Omni."

"What about you, Ruby?" She-Hulk asks, keeping her voice carefully neutral.

She snorts. "Oh, I was tempted. I could unify the six of us without even breaking a guideline, let alone the law. But *you* would be there. Or Thor would, or Spider-Man, or Reed Richards, or Doom, or Kingpin, or… Anyone, really. I don't want to rule the world, Jen. I really don't. Far, *far* too much bother. I'll just keep on being fabulously rich and successful and having a wonderful time. Which reminds me – don't forget to invoice me for this. There'll be a bonus for you too. Both of you."

Achievement: *All's Well That Ends Well.*
Final score: 3 stars.
The end.

286

Jen straightens herself slightly, squaring her shoulders, and marches up to the nearest guard. "Why do we not have VIP passes?" she demands. "This is outrageous. I demand to be let in at once."

The guard looks amused. "And who are you?"

"Jennifer Walters, Thurstech."

He mulls that over, the smirk fading. "One moment, please." He turns away, and mutters into a walkie-talkie. This turns into an ongoing conversation punctuated with lengthy pauses. Finally, he looks back to you. His smirk has returned, and this time it is edged with razors. "You can go on in. Enjoy." Take **+1 {WATCHED}**.

The door buzzes, and you walk through into a small stretch of beige corridor. There are three frosted glass doors at the other end, one directly ahead, the other two set in the walls opposite each other. One is red, another is green, the third blue.

"I've got a bad feeling about this," Jen says. "Which door would you pick?"

"Red." Turn to **194**.

"Green." Turn to **178**.

"Blue." Turn to **298**.

287

"Go for the knee!" you shout.

She-Hulk looks a little surprised, and you're sure you hear her mutter something about arrows, but she shrugs and lunges at the thing, punching it savagely in the side of one knee joint. It doesn't seem phased.

This is a fight!

Round one: roll two dice and add your **POWER** and, if you have any, your **{NOBBLED}**. If the total is 14 or more, you win the first round.

Round two: roll two dice and add your **POWER** and, if you have any, your **{NOBBLED}** and your **{TROUBLESOME}**. If the total is 14 or more, you win the second round.

If you lost both rounds, turn immediately to 7.

Otherwise, the fight ends with the robot broken into scrap. Take **-1 CHARM** and **-2 CONCENTRATION** for the damage She-Hulk took from the vibrosword and the laser cutter., and note the ACHIEVEMENT: *Terminator Too.*

To examine the broken robot, turn to **221**.

To check out the garden, turn to **250**.

288

Hello, what are you doing here? This isn't a place where you should be. This isn't a place at all. Perhaps you're just idly flicking through entries, looking for momentary distraction. Perhaps you're systematically scanning the book, panning for metaphorical gold. Maybe you just kept reading after the robot fight victory at **287**. It's difficult to say, really.

Obviously, this is cheating. Equally obviously, you can't meaningfully cheat at a single-player game unless it stops you having fun.

So, if you like, you may choose to give She-Hulk a careful infusion of gamma rays that means you automatically win every round of every fight. I mean, if you're going to cheat, you might as well *cheat*, y'know? Take the ACHIEVEMENT: *Secret Three.*

There isn't any particular place for you to go from here, except back to wherever it was you came from. Go for it!

289

The bench misses Chtylok, and as the fight progresses, the creature seems to get a few solid blows in. She-Hulk appears to be slowing.

Arcade yammers on continually from the sidelines like a sports commentator, but you're ignoring him.

There's a loud crunch just a short distance behind you, and you whip round to see the Thing burst through the arena wall. He looks at the fight, nods to you, then glances at a watch. "Yeah, that's the signal. I made it in … 53 seconds. Not bad. Anything I need to know so far, friend?"

Is that all? It feels like the fight's been going for ages. "It's incredibly strong," you say.

You both wince as She-Hulk is hammered into the arena wall again.

"Got it," the Thing says. He sprints into the fray, and exchanges a few words with She-Hulk who grabs him, and jumps. A moment later, they're clinging to the feathers either side of Chtylok's head.

"*Kraw!*" it roars.

Make a clobbering test for Jen and Ben. Roll two dice, add your **POWER** twice, and subtract your {WOBBLY} once.

> Get to 21 or more: turn to **106**.
>
> 20 or less: turn to **265**.

Chtylok was the last obstacle in Arcade's maze. You track the fiend down to a comfortable boardroom not far from the arena. He's in the large executive chair you saw on the monitors, at the head of a huge meeting table. There are plenty laptops in front of various seats, but no people.

As you walk in, Arcade stands and bows sarcastically, applauding. "Well *done*," he says. "You beat the unstoppable monster. I'm going to have to kill that xenologist… but I suppose you must have some questions."

"Only one," She-Hulk rumbles. "Are you coming quietly, or do I get to punch you?"

Add your **CHARM** and {**SIMPATICO**} together, and if the total is less than 10, turn to **260** now.

Still here? What is your {**WAVES**} score?

5 or more: turn to **210**.

4 or less: turn to **205**.

291

The cloakroom is, well, a cloakroom. A big space for hanging coats and jackets, along with a small attendant's station, currently empty, and a sort of reception zone for people to wait in. Across the reception zone is a sturdy looking oak door with a red light above it and a big keypad to one side. The entry to the secure suite!

You head over there. Jen tries the code Ruby gave her, but unsurprisingly, it doesn't work.

This is a puzzle!

Look at the following numbers: *51, 67, 85, 119, 153.*

One of them is the odd one out. Turn to an entry that matches the number you picked, and if the first words you see are not "This is the odd one out!", turn instead to **195**.

Alternatively, you can take a penalty and bypass the puzzle by turning to **29**.

292

The parlor turns out to be a small, comfy-looking living space. The couch and armchair look comfy, there's a laptop on a coffee table, a big TV with several current-generation games consoles beneath it, and a scattering of computer enthusiast magazines. The decoration appears to be mostly made up of framed cells from animated movies – you clearly recognize the *Akira* and *Spirited Away* panels – and figurines of prominent heroes and villains are scattered here and there. The room is free of both red-lit doors and unlikely lunatics.

Jen checks her floorplan. "Dining room or spa?"

For the dining room, turn to **3**.

For the spa, turn to **137**.

293

"You got it," Jen says. She tenses, and as Walrus approaches, she springs at him. Walrus grunts and steps aside with far more speed than you'd expect, swinging the hammer as he does so. You hear a brutal-sounding crunch, and She-Hulk lands on the fake pool several feet away, groaning. "Ow," she says. She doesn't sound happy. "I'm not," she adds, frowning. "I thought Deadpool dealt with that damn hammer."

Walrus turns and lumbers toward her deceptively fast. She rolls, and the hammer misses her head to crack the floor alarmingly. She-Hulk flips back to her feet, then goes in for a punch.

This is one round of an extended fight. Roll two dice, add your **POWER**, and subtract your {**PENALTY**}. If you have [**Spiked Knuckles**], add 2. What's your total?

On a 12 or more: Turn to **222**.

11 or less: Turn to **120**.

294

Jen securely ties Ringmaster down, blindfolded and gagged and facing into a corner. Once he's restrained, she turns to his companion. "You too, Professor."

"Yes, ma'am," the little guy says glumly. He holds his hands out, and she binds them, then ties him to a table across the room from his boss.

It only takes a moment more to open Ruby's files and download the video recording which definitively shows her here, in this room, on a call with a bunch of independent witnesses, at the time of Bright's death.

While She-Hulk is getting the file, you spot an interesting [Chrome Bracelet] bristling with electronics on the inside and featuring multiple skin sensors. You may take it with you: while it is in your inventory, take +2 CONCENTRATION.

With the file duplicated onto two separate USB drives, She-Hulk turns to the Professor. "Who's behind this?" she growls.

"I don't know," he replies. He sounds depressed and sincere. "I don't think even Maynard knows for sure. But I do know that we're just one cog in a very big, complex operation. There are people all across Silicon Valley, and we've all been paid very generously for last week and this week. The contract winds up Sunday evening. Whoever is behind this, they've got a lot of money and a great sense of spectacle."

"And what were *you* supposed to do?"

"Just keep this mansion locked down. See off anyone who came sniffing around."

Jen nods. "I thought it was something like that. Thanks." Take +1 {WHEELS WITHIN WHEELS}. Ringmaster's top hat is in a corner. She goes over to it, then stomps it enthusiastically into a purple mess. By the time she's finished you can't even see any fragments of hypnotic disk. ACHIEVEMENT: *Mad Hat*.

Jen calls the police, making sure to warn them that the mansion is only partly secured and there's a bunch of thugs still on the loose. What do you suggest doing while you wait for them?

Research Ruby's case using her computers? Turn to
133.
Call Ruby and fill her in on the situation. Turn to
281.

295

With Oort unconscious and Big Wheel's wheel melted
down to scrap by Ruby's energy beams, things gradually
begin to calm down. It's another hour before the villains
are safely in the custody of the authorities. Miraculously, no
one was killed, but several people have been hospitalized,
and Ruby has a nasty burn across one shoulder.

She declines to seek treatment, however, and the three
of you retreat down the street to a café with a private room
that opens magically to her ebony credit card. "Tell me
about Tekeli," she says.

"Pattern recognition systems built using alien tissue," Jen
says. "I have footage." She shows Ruby the clip she took of
the space lab computer systems.

"That's it," Ruby says unhappily. "Total global information control."

"It's got to be stopped," Jen declares.

"I was supposed to be in jail this weekend, but everyone
else load-bearing in the six companies is going to be at
ElectroCon LA. Whoever is behind this, he thinks that by
the end of the Expo, he'll have everything he needs."

"Then that's where we have to be."

"I'm not the frontal assault type,' Ruby says. 'I'm going

to drop into the background. I prefer working behind the scenes anyway."

Jen nods. "That makes sense."

To ask what Ruby means by "load-bearing" people, turn to **158**.

To ask about total information control, turn to **172**.

296

Exie sighs. "He was full of life. So many tech guru types are all twisted up, consumed by various obsessions, but Sturm was a fun guy, *and* he bathed daily. He was half-Swedish, and I think that gave him a very companionable outlook on life. He was as sharp as a razor beneath it, his mind was always working out how things went together. You'd never notice it if you were having a beer with him in a bar somewhere, though. He hated making people feel dumb. I miss him. The world is emptier without him."

Do you have {**SENSELESS**} of 1? If so, discussion turns to possible motivations for the murder. "He'd become very interested by one of Tekeli Industries' projects in the days leading up to his death. He'd been talking to them before, but he'd learned something new. That's the only thing I can think of." Take **+2 {REASONABLE DOUBT}**.

Now, to ask about the murder, turn to **138**.

To go visit Ruby in jail finally, turn to **89**.

297

"As you like," Jen says. "I'll try not to hurt them too much."

She advances on the bouncing twins. They leap to flank her, and attempt a tricksy move that clearly doesn't work, because it ends with each of them ferociously trying to grapple one of her arms. She-Hulk brings her hands together sharply, their stupid heads smack together, and they slide to the floor. Take **+1 {INTENSITY}**.

Jen checks them over. "I think they're OK. They're not unconscious, at least. That's the important thing." She looks at you seriously. "Knocking people out is really dangerous. Even a fist fight can easily prove fatal."

"Right," you say. "I'm not really the knocking-people-out type."

"Oh, I know *you're* not," she says breezily. "Anyway, from here, we can try the library or the cloakroom."

"The library." Turn to **64**.

"The cloakroom." Turn to **291**.

298

You pass through the blue door into… darkness. Even the door behind you has seemingly vanished. A moment later, fans start up around the room, although you don't feel any draft.

"I think I get the picture," Jen says. She reaches out and places a hand on your arm. "Stay close." She starts walking, and you hear her other hand brushing the wall.

As you progress, you note that it seems to be getting colder. It's tiring. You're starting to feel a little out of breath, too. Make a resilience test. Roll one die and add your Power. If the total is 8 or less, take -1 CONCENTRATION.

Then it clicks. "They're pumping the air out," you say.

"Nasty," Jen says. You hear a loud crack, and light blooms through the fist-sized hole she just punched in the wall. Air hisses back in rapidly. In the dim light, you can see a couple of doors across the room. One is marked with a badge, the other with a lectern.

For the badge door, turn to **170**.

For the lectern door, turn to **183**.

The coffee room is suspiciously straight-forward. It's small and bland, with cheap flooring, and could be a refreshment station in any corporate environment – a plain sideboard holds a coffee jug on a heated plate, a kettle, some bags of tea and sugar, a stack of creamer pots, and some mugs decorated with an old-time arcade machine. A chipped sink with a single tap is next to it. There's a simple table against the other wall holding a microwave. Finally, opposite the door you came in by, there's another door with a sign saying *"Arena: Combatants Only."*

Jen looks at everything suspiciously. She sniffs the coffee and the kettle, turns on the tap, opens some of the packets, and tastes some of the items. Finally, she shrugs. "This could just as easily have been a decent espresso machine. Honestly, it's the little things that get to you. Still, it seems harmless."

If you want to have a mug of coffee or tea, make a note that you did so.

"Come on now. Are we ready to see what joys the Arena has for us?" She-Hulk asks.

"Sure." Turn to **197**.

"Let's check the washroom first." Turn to **26**.

300

If you were hoping to find the final entry here, unfortunately your victory is in another castle. We humbly suggest that you'll have more fun if you start at entry 1 and play through the book the way it's designed. It's a lot more fun that way, we promise.

If you're here as part of your investigation into Vanguard, well done! Take the ACHIEVEMENT: *Cracked.*

You enter a corridor with polished wooden floors and off-white walls, decorated sparsely with paintings of futuristic cityscapes. It all looks suspiciously normal. There are simple wooden doors at each end of the corridor with nothing much to distinguish them, except that there's a faint draft of fresh air coming from the door to the right.

She-Hulk looks at you expectantly.

"Let's go left." Turn to **127**.

"Let's go right." Turn to **206**.

ACHIEVEMENTS CHECKLIST

As you find these ACHIEVEMENTS in play, check them off the list!

- ☐ *All's Well That Ends Well*
- ☐ *Bouncing Matilda*
- ☐ *Bringing Down the House*
- ☐ *Brownout*
- ☐ *By the Skin of Your Teeth*
- ☐ *Clean Sweep*
- ☐ *Clippy*
- ☐ *Cosmic Tunnel*
- ☐ *Cracked*
- ☐ *Dazzled*
- ☐ *Falling at the First Hurdle*
- ☐ *Gumshoe*
- ☐ *Improbable*
- ☐ *It Goes Up to 11*
- ☐ *It's Doric Time*
- ☐ *It's Murderworld All the Way Down*
- ☐ *Just Like a Toothpaste Tube*
- ☐ *Just Too Much*
- ☐ *Keep Turning Left*
- ☐ *Lost in Space*
- ☐ *Mad Hat*
- ☐ *Menacing Doodads*
- ☐ *Mooooo*
- ☐ *My Watermelon Impression*
- ☐ *Not So Cool Now, Huh?*
- ☐ *Puppet Masters*
- ☐ *Riddled*
- ☐ *Rubygeddon*
- ☐ *Secret One*
- ☐ *Secret Two*
- ☐ *Secret Three*
- ☐ *Secret Four*
- ☐ *Secret Five*
- ☐ *Secret Six*
- ☐ *Sip of Faith*
- ☐ *Smashing*
- ☐ *So Near and Yet So Far*
- ☐ *Suspicious Minds*
- ☐ *Teamwork*
- ☐ *Terminator Too*
- ☐ *That Tickles*
- ☐ *The End of the World Again*
- ☐ *The Experimentalist*
- ☐ *The Odd One*
- ☐ *This is for the Oysters*
- ☐ *Virtue is its Own Reward*

SUPER-ACHIEVEMENTS CHECKLIST

- ☐ Finish with a combined **POWER + CHARM + CONCENTRATION** of 20 or more: *Mighty.*
- ☐ Finish with at least two stars and a combined **POWER + CHARM + CONCENTRATION** of 5 or less: *Cutting it Close.*
- ☐ Finish with 1 or 0 stars: *Whoops, Apocalypse.*
- ☐ Finish with {**WAVES**} of 10 or more: *Agents of Chaos.*
- ☐ Finish with {**SIMPATICO**} of 0: *Frenemy.*
- ☐ Finish with {**SIMPATICO**} of 5 or more: *Beautiful Beginnings.*
- ☐ Finish with {**PUZZLER**} of 5 or more: *Brilliant.*
- ☐ Finish with {**LEGAL FAVOR**} of 1: *I'll Take That to Go.*
- ☐ Finish without cheating even once: *Moral Powerhouse.*
- ☐ Finish with a [**Chrome Bracelet**], [**Sinister Medallion**], [**Experimental Gauntlet**], [**Crystal Dodecahedron**], and [**Glowing Pearl**]: *Leveled Up.*
- ☐ Finish with any five from [**Abomination Wire**], [**Coffee**], [**Glop**], [**Hot Chocolate**], [**Mysterious Skull**], [**Sports Drink**], and [**Triple Espresso**]: *Pack Rat.*
- ☐ Discover all 28 items across various playthroughs: *The 100% Run.*
- ☐ Discover all 5 starred endings: *Determined.*
- ☐ Discover all 8 deaths: *Messy.*
- ☐ Discover all 6 Secret achievements: *Eagle-Eyed.*
- ☐ Collect all 16 super-achievements above this one: *Thorough.*
- ☐ Collect all 46 in-text achievements: *Perfectionist.*
- ☐ And if you collect both *Thorough* and *Perfectionist*: award yourself *You're Sensational!*

ABOUT THE AUTHOR

TIM DEDOPULOS is an unrepentant writer, editor, puzzle creator, game designer, and all-round word-slinger. He has written and/or edited just about everything it is possible to get paid to write and/or edit – books, manuals, games, puzzles, billboards, scripts, slogans, contracts, yadda yadda yadda – except plays. So far. He has used about a dozen pen-names which must remain absolutely secret. A long-time lover of science fiction, fantasy, horror, and comics, he is particularly interested in the places where prose, film and game are coming together. He can be found on Twitter as *@ghostwoods*, where he exclusively tweets absolute nonsense and insists on pretending the real world isn't happening.

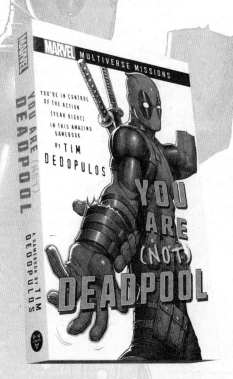

WORLD EXPANDING FICTION

Do you have them all?

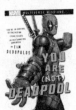

Marvel Crisis Protocol
☐ *Target: Kree* by Stuart Moore
☐ *Shadow Avengers* by Carrie Harris

Marvel Heroines
☐ *Domino: Strays* by Tristan Palmgren
☐ *Rogue: Untouched* by Alisa Kwitney
☐ *Elsa Bloodstone: Bequest* by Cath Lauria
☐ *Outlaw: Relentless* by Tristan Palmgren
☐ *Black Cat: Discord* by Cath Lauria
☐ *Squirrel Girl: Universe* by Tristan Palmgren *(coming soon)*

Legends of Asgard
☐ *The Head of Mimir* by Richard Lee Byers
☐ *The Sword of Surtur* by C L Werner
☐ *The Serpent and the Dead* by Anna Stephens
☐ *The Rebels of Vanaheim* by Richard Lee Byers
☐ *Three Swords* by C L Werner
☐ *The Prisoner of Tartarus* by Richard Lee Byers *(coming soon)*

Multiverse Missions
☐ *You Are (Not) Deadpool* by Tim Dedopulos
☑ *She-Hulk Goes to Murderworld* by Tim Dedopulos

School of X
☐ *The Siege of X-41* by Tristan Palmgren
☐ *Sound of Light* by Amanda Bridgeman *(coming soon)*

Marvel Untold
☐ *The Harrowing of Doom* by David Annandale
☐ *Dark Avengers: The Patriot List* by David Guymer
☐ *Witches Unleashed* by Carrie Harris
☐ *Reign of the Devourer* by David Annandale
☐ *Sisters of Sorcery* by Marsheila Rockwell *(coming soon)*

Xavier's Institute
☐ *Liberty & Justice for All* by Carrie Harris
☐ *First Team* by Robbie MacNiven
☐ *Triptych* by Jaleigh Johnson
☐ *School of X* edited by Gwendolyn Nix

**EXPLORE OUR WORLD
EXPANDING FICTION**

ACONYTEBOOKS.COM
@ACONYTEBOOKS
ACONYTEBOOKS.COM/NEWSLETTER